ADVENTURE

LAUNCHED FROM THE CASTLE

•

PETER REESE DOYLE

FOCUS ON THE FAMILY

PUBLISHING

Colorado Springs, Colorado

Library of Congress Cataloging-in-Publication Data
Doyle, Peter Reese, 1930–

    LAUNCHED FROM THE CASTLE / Peter Reese Doyle.

    p. cm—(Daring Family adventures; bk. 7)

  Summary: While in Germany with their father, Mark and Penny Daring and their friend David become involved in trying to figure out how a fortune in jewels was stolen from a well-protected castle.

    ISBN 1-56179-368-X
  [1. Adventure and adventurers—Fiction. 2. Brothers and sisters—Fiction.

  3. Germany—Fiction.] I. Title. II. Series: Doyle, Peter Reese, 1930– Daring

Family adventures; bk. 7.

PZ7.D777Lau 1995

[Fic]—dc20   95-2694

                                               CIP

                                             AC

Published by Focus on the Family Publishing, Colorado Springs,
Colorado 80995.

Distributed in the U.S. and Canada by Word Books, Dallas, Texas.

Editor: Deena Davis
Cover Design: James A. Lebbad
Cover Illustration: Ken Spengler

Printed in the United States of America

95 96 97 98 99/10 9 8 7 6 5 4 3 2 1

*For
Miss Betty Thomas,
a teacher of good things
(Titus 2:1,3–5)*

CONTENTS

CHAPTER 1

BIRDS OF PREY

There was no moon.

The huge bulk of the ancient castle loomed above the village, its ramparts a barely discernible smudge in the black summer night.

One by one, the four men in their hang gliders ran toward the edge of the high castle wall and launched themselves into the dark. Clearing the walls and the hill on which Castle Königstein stood, the gliders swerved left, turning in a graceful circle until they pointed southeast.

Kurt led the flight. The second man had turned his glider slightly to Kurt's left, the third flew to his right. The fourth followed directly behind Kurt some 40 yards back. The loose diamond formation soared across fields, borne swiftly and silently by the strong wind, toward Joseph Braun's villa just two miles away.

In the distance, the Taunus Mountains towered over the intervening plains, but the darkness made the mountains invisible to the men in the gliders.

1

Kurt led them by compass and by the clusters of lights from farmhouses below. For the past several days, he'd studied these lighted houses from the castle walls, plotting the course with care to avoid passing over homes and other buildings. He wanted them to fly as much as possible over the fields and forests that lay between them and their target.

Back in the castle, three cursing men struggled to dismantle the hang glider that had been accidentally damaged just before the flight. The left wing had snagged a projection from the stone wall of the tunnel, ripping the fabric, and a vital tubular frame of the wing had been bent. The craft was useless until it could be repaired.

"You fool!" the stocky man hissed to Eric on his right as they took the wings off the glider. "Eric, how did you wreck this thing? We practiced this over and over!"

"I never saw that stone sticking out from that wall," Eric replied defensively. "I kept telling you we should have used lights to get these gliders out of the tunnel. No one could see us from the village."

"Kurt said 'no lights'!" Stefan retorted. "That's why we practiced each night. The others launched theirs without trouble!"

"What does it matter now?" the lean man behind them asked. "We also practiced the drill to follow if one of these gliders got damaged. The men who launched know what to do. Let's quit arguing and get the glider back into the cave. We've got to get out of this castle as soon as Kurt and the others reach the villa!"

They carried the dismantled craft back inside the castle,

turned to the right into a tunnel, and dragged the glider toward the back of a room at the end.

"How long can we leave this stuff here before we have to come back and cart it away?" Eric asked.

"We've got six more days," Stefan replied. "The castle's closed that long for repairs, according to the signs!"

The men laughed. Those signs were part of their elaborate plan to keep tourists out of Castle Königstein, and they would continue to keep them out until the gang's arrangements had been completed, their equipment removed, and all signs of their use of this historic fortress carefully swept away. The manager of the castle had been paid well for not asking why the group wished to use the fortress. He'd complied readily, spreading the news to the tourist bureau in the town and putting up signs. The disappointed tourists who flocked regularly to this historic site were none the wiser.

Kurt and his men had brought their gliders and the rest of their equipment to the castle in a large truck and had carried everything inside the massive stone structure. Dressed as workers, they had prowled the grounds for several days, setting up their radios and practicing for the raid. By day and by night, they'd studied the course they would fly to Herr Braun's villa. Each evening, they'd spent a great deal of time plotting their course to avoid the lights from farmhouses dotting the landscape between the castle and the villa.

The east wall of the ancient castle towered above the cliff on which it was perched, giving gliders plenty of drop room for launching.

"Here's how we'll do it," Kurt told them the first day they

were there. "We'll run along this wall and launch there." He pointed. "We'll swing left in a gradual circle, then settle on our course for the villa. You'll each have compasses with luminous dials. But you won't need them; just follow me by the lights on the tips of my wings. They're aimed backward—you can see them, but no one from the ground can. We've practiced these night flights for two years; this will be a snap."

Kurt pointed toward the villa, then moved his arm to the left. "See those fields? We'll cross them to avoid the houses and then veer back over that cluster of trees and through that forest. The dark will keep anyone from seeing us, but we still won't take chances."

After bringing the damaged glider to the storeroom at the end of the narrow passage, the men pulled out their flashlights and set the craft against the wall. A thick tarpaulin covered the window that looked over the valley so no one would spot their lights. Eric turned on the radio where Heinz huddled.

"How's it going?" Eric asked anxiously, disappointed that he'd damaged his glider and missed the attack.

"Excellent, Kurt says!" Heinz replied. "The wind is perfect. They're halfway there."

These men had worked and trained together for the past two years. It was not the first raid they'd launched, but if they pulled it off, it would be the biggest. The treasure they planned to lift from Herr Braun's villa was fabulous: a huge load of jewels from Anatole Navarre's famous shop in Paris!

Joseph Braun lived and held court in the villa that his family had owned for three hundred years. Shielded on two sides

by thick forest, guarded on the other sides by farms, and surrounded completely by a ten-foot-high stone wall, the villa
was as safe a place as a multimillionaire could hope to afford.
Some of the farm buildings were very old indeed, but they'd
been extensively modernized. Elaborate security systems
guarded the perimeter of the eight-acre plot, as well as the
buildings inside the walls.

There were only two gates in the walls of the villa, one at
the north, the other at the south, with a guardhouse at each.
The central security office was housed in the basement of one
of the buildings. Manned at all times by Herr Braun's elite
security force, the electronic system allowed no opportunity
for unauthorized intrusion. No one—absolutely no one—
entered Herr Braun's villa without his permission.

The generator that powered the security system was housed
next to the office of the security director, a former intelligence
officer in the new Luftwaffe. An interruption of the villa's elec-
tric power would not affect the electronic security system,
which was always on alert. Braun's place was impregnable.

Inside the rambling house at the top of the hill, Herr
Braun's party was in full swing. The genial host had just led
the cheerful guests into the showpiece that was his living
room. Happily full from a fabulous meal, the couples wandered in, laughing and chatting, and sank into the luxurious
chairs and sofas. Everyone was elegantly dressed as befitted
the occasion, for it was Herr Braun's birthday. This was the
annual party he threw for his friends.

Herr Braun had always staged an elaborate entertainment
for these wealthy friends. This year he had contacted all the

men and secured their agreement to participate in giving a real surprise to their wives. The surprise was a valuable, glittering collection of jewelry from the shop of Anatole Navarre of Paris.

Joseph Braun stood by the grand piano and addressed his guests. "This year, ladies, your husbands have refused to allow me to present you with entertainment. They have insisted on participating in the surprise themselves. Let me introduce you to the famous jewel merchant from Paris, Monsieur Anatole Navarre!"

The ladies cried out in surprise and pleasure as the dignified merchant walked into the room followed by three carts of multitiered trays of jewels pushed by dark-suited assistants.

"Monsieur Navarre has brought a marvelous collection for you to choose from, ladies," Joseph Braun continued. "Your husbands have had months to save for this occasion." Everyone laughed at this; not one of these rich men needed to save a penny.

As the ladies rushed over to the carts, the assistants pulled out side trays that glowed and sparkled with the jewelry for which Anatole Navarre's shop was famous. Necklaces, rings, bracelets, pins—the assortment was fabulous. And fabulously expensive. The men grinned with pleasure at the joy this surprise had brought their wives.

"It's Ladies' Night!" Herr Braun said. "Choose what you wish! Your husbands will pay for it!"

"Within reason, of course," the corpulent banker Herr Schliemann called out in mock alarm.

Everyone laughed. Herr Schliemann was the richest man

in the room, and one of the richest men in the city of Frankfurt.

"By the way, Joseph," Schliemann continued, "are you sure all these jewels are safe in your home?"

Everyone laughed again. It was well known that Herr Braun's extensive security system, with his professional team of guards, was probably the most elaborate of any nonmilitary system in the country.

"His security's better than mine!" General Dietrich, head of the Luftwaffe's fighter wing, called out. He added, "I wish the government would give *me* the equipment Joseph has guarding his home! We couldn't be safer anywhere in the world! Nothing can get in here—not even a field mouse— without a personal invitation from Joseph."

The crowd loved it. They all knew this was true. That's why they felt so safe with the trays of jewels spread all over the living room.

"This place is impregnable!" General Dietrich insisted again.

Three hundred yards away, the hang gliders swooped toward their target, the wind barely whispering through their wings. In the lead, Kurt spoke into the radio strapped to his wrist.

Back at the castle, Eric replied. So did the gray-clad guard inside the control center of Herr Braun's security system. This guard took out a small black box and slid back the thin metal top exposing a red button. Then he nodded to the man beside him. Picking up two canisters of nerve gas, the man pulled on his mask and left the room, pressing a button on the wall as he did so. In three parts of the house, other men heard their instruments buzz. They, too, picked up their canisters, put on their masks, and moved into position.

As the gliders approached the wall of Herr Braun's villa, Kurt spoke one word into the radio strapped to his wrist: "Execute!"

The guard by the generator flipped the red button on the small black box, and all the lights and power went out through Herr Braun's entire estate.

So did the security system.

CHAPTER 2

FRANKFURT

The Lufthansa jet approached the runway and touched down smoothly. The powerful engines switched into reverse, and the massive craft shuddered as its speed dropped rapidly. The plane began to turn toward the terminal.

"Boy!" David exclaimed. "Are we getting to see Germany this summer! First Düsseldorf, now Frankfurt."

"And Egypt, too," Penny added. She sat at the window. David was to her left, and Penny's brother, Mark, sat across the aisle.

"Don't forget France," Mark added. "Egypt and France and Germany—all in one summer!"

David Curtis was 17, Mark's age, and a year older than Penny. David was tall, lean, and broad-shouldered. He and Mark obviously worked out and were in tip-top condition. David had come to visit Mark and Penny Daring at their home in East Africa, where Mr. Daring owned and managed an engineering firm. But they'd traveled more than they had expected.

They'd spent almost a week in Egypt, then they'd gone to Paris, then to the south of France. They'd been in Germany less than a week and were flying into Frankfurt this day to help Mr. Daring with a project his firm was handling for a French-German business group.

At five feet eleven, Mark was two inches shorter than David, and more massively built. The two had been great friends for years. Penny was five feet seven, slender, with light brown hair and the prettiest brown eyes David had ever seen.

The boys wore polo shirts and slacks. Penny wore a light summer dress. They were all excited at the prospect of visiting this important German city.

"We'll be here for just five days," Mark observed as the plane reached the terminal and people prepared to stand and retrieve their bags.

"Well, your father said we could work for him each morning and then explore the city in the afternoons," David reminded him. "We'll get to see a lot!"

"How will we recognize Herr Schultz?" Penny asked, always the practical one. "He's never seen us and we've never seen him."

"Don't worry, Penny," David insisted. "With my command of the German language, I'll just go ask every man in the terminal if his name is Schultz. We can't miss him."

"We'll be here a week if you do that!" she said, laughing. She shouldered her camera case and followed Mark down the aisle to the door.

"Actually," David corrected himself, "Herr Schultz will find *us*. Your father told him to look for a very pretty girl who's escorted by a young man in top condition, along with a big, out-of-shape, puffy American boy. He'll recognize us at once!"

"We'll see who's out of shape when we practice karate tomorrow!" Mark warned.

But spot them Herr Schultz did. As they walked into the terminal, a tall, dark-haired man in a dark suit approached and showed them his card. His blue eyes twinkled in his wide face as he introduced himself.

"I'm Herr Schultz, and you are Mark and Penny and David, I believe!" he said with a smile. They shook his hand, happy to have found him so quickly. "Follow me; we'll get your bags. Then I'll drive you home."

In a short while, he was driving them through the busy traffic of Frankfurt, telling them about the various buildings they passed. "Your father was called suddenly to Berlin," he told them. "He'll be back in two days. But he's left some work for you to do, 'so you won't get bored,' he said."

"Boy, it's been a long time since we've been bored *this* summer!" Mark observed.

"He's left his laptop computer for you, Penny," Herr Schultz continued. "And he's got some more French for you and Mark to translate. It's all written down at his desk."

"Great!" David said. "I'll just borrow Penny's camera, wander around Frankfurt, and see the sights."

"I'm afraid not, David," Herr Schultz replied with a twinkle in his eye. "He's got some German documents for you to translate so Penny can type them into the laptop."

Mark and Penny laughed as David pretended to scowl.

"It's high time David worked on this trip," Mark said emphatically.

"It sure is!" Penny agreed. "All he's done so far this summer is eat himself into a stupor and get Mark and me into trouble. It's been awful, Herr Schultz! You wouldn't believe the trouble he's stirred up!"

Herr Schultz could tell from the sparkle in her eyes that Penny had loved every minute of David's company that summer.

"Yes, I would, Penny," Herr Schultz said smiling. "Your father told me of the adventures you three have had these past several weeks. He said you've packed a lifetime into less than two months!"

They all laughed at that. Herr Schultz continued, "He also told me to remind you to be very alert."

"But there's no danger to Dad's firm here in Frankfurt, is there, Herr Schultz?" Mark asked in surprise.

"We don't think so, Mark," Herr Schultz replied. "But with all the things that have happened so far, he just wants you three to keep your eyes open. After all, there's an immense treasure in those ancient Egyptian tombs your father's firm is excavating, and you know how people have already tried to steal it."

Just then he turned the Mercedes into a driveway and parked. They got out, and he helped the boys get the bags from the trunk. David carried Penny's luggage along with his own as Herr Schultz led them into his house.

Frau Schultz was tall like her husband, with a friendly face and sparkling blue eyes. She welcomed the Americans warmly and led Penny to her room while her husband showed the boys where they would stay. The three teenagers unpacked their bags and hung up their clothes before going downstairs again.

"Here are some messages from your father," Frau Schultz told Mark and Penny. "And David, there's some mail from your family in the United States."

"Great!" David exclaimed, taking the letters she handed him. "I hope they got the mail I sent them from Düsseldorf."

"You can relax for an hour, if you like," Herr Schultz said from the hall. "Later we'll go into town for dinner and show you some of the sights of the city."

"This will be a wonderful vacation!" Penny exclaimed, her eyes shining with pleasure.

Mark grinned. "It's high time we had one!" he said emphatically.

David was immersed in his sister's letter and didn't hear them.

CHAPTER 3

"DID YOU HEAR THE NEWS?"

That evening, the Schultzes took the three to downtown Frankfurt.

"We're going to eat at a most unusual place," Frau Schultz told them. "There's not another store like this in Germany. It's Swiss-owned, and it's a very modern department store with a nice restaurant. You can see people from all over the world passing by as you eat."

"What's the name of the restaurant, Frau Schultz?" Penny asked eagerly. Already she and the boys felt very much at home with this friendly couple.

"It's called Marché, Penny," Frau Schultz replied. "It has a sloping walkway that goes up inside the building. You pass all the different stores as you climb. Or we can take the elevator. Each store has a different decor, and all of them are so colorful. You'll love it!"

"Wonderful!" Penny said, eyes shining. "I'll get some good photos." Penny was a serious and very competent photographer.

"I'm afraid you can't take pictures inside the building, Penny," Frau Schultz told her. "The design of the store is so modern and unusual—and so successful—that they don't want people copying it. They don't want their competition to have any advantage."

Herr Schultz parked the car and they began to walk through the wide pedestrian walkways of downtown Frankfurt.

"These used to be streets for cars," Herr Schultz told them, "but they've changed that. Now cars are kept out, so there's lots of room for pedestrians. Many places in Germany have done this."

Suddenly, they came to a stop. A crowd of people in front of them were gathered around nine dancers and singers dressed in bright red costumes.

"They're from Romania, I believe," Frau Schultz told them.

"Keep a tight grip on your purses, ladies!" her husband reminded them. "Thieves and pickpockets sometimes prowl among crowds at night!"

They watched the dancers for a while. Then Herr Schultz stepped forward and tossed a five-mark coin into a basket on the ground. Others had done the same and continued to do so as the group sang and danced.

"This is how many singers and dancers make part of their living," Frau Schultz told the Americans. "We'll see lots of people performing downtown like this."

Herr Schultz led them past a large building with a rounded front on the corner of a pedestrian intersection. Next to this building was Marché. David got just a glimpse of seven or eight floors before they went inside and walked down the steps to the level below.

There, to their right, was the restaurant. Brightly lit and cheerfully decorated, it was half full. The Americans looked around at the counters of food on the various levels.

"Look!" Penny exclaimed suddenly, pointing to a section of wall with tables and chairs set inside. "Those are pictures of Greece . . . and the Mediterranean. How charming!"

"I think that's one of the reasons this place is so popular," Herr Schultz said smiling. "Germans seem to be surrounded by dark skies and dark colors all the time—especially in winter. I think these bright Mediterranean colors appeal to us.

"Let's look around first and see what they've got on the different counters. Then choose what you wish. But save room for dessert; they've got some splendid German chocolate you won't want to miss."

"Oh, the boys are on a diet, Herr Schultz," Penny replied with a straight face. "They're so fat and overweight. But I'd love some chocolate."

The Schultzes laughed, then led them to several counters. They all finally chose a lamb dish with vegetables and went through the checkout line.

"Let's sit by this Mediterranean scene," Herr Schultz said, leading them back to the corner nearest the door. There, through a large glass wall, they had an excellent view of the people passing by as well as of shops along the inclined walkway.

They all had coffee when they finished dinner.

"Let me tell you tomorrow's schedule," their host said. "After breakfast I'll take you to my office, and you can start on those projects for your father. He'll fax me from Berlin and let me know when he's returning. My engineers are working on the documents he brought us from Paris, and we've got some questions he said you'd be able to answer for us. Then I'll take you to lunch—back here, if you like. But there's been a change of plans."

He paused and looked at the eager teenagers, a gleam in his eye. "Your father, Mark and Penny, wants to bring some more documentation back from Berlin before you three do too much work on the material we have here. If you like, you can work at the office after lunch and probably finish what's there. Then you could spend the whole of the next day exploring an old castle—if you don't think that would be too boring!"

"Boring! We'd love it, Herr Schultz!" Mark said excitedly, and Penny and David agreed emphatically.

"Splendid! You can borrow Frau Schultz's car after breakfast and drive a short way to the town of Königstein. There's a fabulous eleventh-century castle there. It happens to be closed for some repairs right now, but it's owned by a friend of mine. When I told him I wanted you to see some interesting sights in our country, he gladly volunteered to contact the castle manager and let you three have a private visit. You could spend several hours there, eat at a fine restaurant—a very old one, in fact—then return in the afternoon."

The three Americans were ecstatic. A private visit to an eleventh-century German castle!

"The place is very interesting," Herr Schultz continued. "It's huge. Walls surround a large area around the building. Different levels of fortifications rise to the top of the hill. You can climb the steps to the top of the tall tower and see for great distances. If it's a clear day, Penny, you'll get some wonderful pictures!"

Suddenly, Frau Schultz interrupted her husband. "Carl, did you hear the news today?" she asked, her face grave.

"No," he replied, puzzled at her tone.

"Joseph Braun's villa was robbed last night while a large group of very wealthy guests was there. He was having a party. Monsieur Navarre, the Paris jeweler, had brought a very valuable display of gems for Joseph's guests. And they were all stolen!"

"Impossible!" her husband replied, astounded at the news. "Everyone knows that Joseph has the finest security system money can buy! It's as good as the military has, they say. No one can get inside that villa without Joseph's personal permission!"

"But someone got in last night," she insisted. "The news says that the whole security system was shut off. The Brauns and their guests were put to sleep with some kind of gas, and the thieves drove out the gate with a vanload of jewels worth millions of marks!"

"Have they found the thieves?" her husband asked incredulously.

"Not yet," she said. "But they had an accident as they drove away from the villa. Their van was hit by a car driven by a drunk driver and knocked off the road. The thieves took what they could carry—a fortune!—and ran into the woods."

"Well, they won't get away, then," Herr Schultz said. "The police can quickly round them up if they're on foot."

"But they haven't yet," she said. "They're not saying much about it, but the news people speculate there's a real mystery here the police can't fathom. And there's another thing," she added. "Apparently, some of the thieves took a truck and drove in the opposite direction, to the north. Some people heard that truck, but no one identified it properly, and they don't know where it went."

"Poor Joseph!" Herr Schultz said, shaking his head sadly. "How he bragged about that security system! His whole villa has a tall stone wall around it with electronic sensors all over. He's got his own private security force—they're professionals, all former military. Who would have thought that *anyone* could break into that place?"

The Schultzes changed the subject then and began to tell the three Americans about the city of Frankfurt. Mark, Penny, and David were excited about the prospect of being there, of working on Mr. Daring's fascinating Egyptian "project," and of exploring Castle Königstein the day after next.

CHAPTER 4

THE MYSTERY AT CASTLE KÖNIGSTEIN

Two days later, Mark, Penny, and David left the city of Frankfurt in Frau Schultz's gray Opel sedan. David drove, Penny sat beside him, and Mark was in the back. They were excited at the prospect of exploring an ancient castle all by themselves.

"What a beautiful countryside!" Penny exclaimed happily, as they left the busy city on the wide highway and headed into the country toward the village of Königstein.

"I can't get over how clean the German cities and roads are," Mark said. "There's no trash littering the land, no dilapidated buildings falling down by the side of the road. These people really like to keep things neat."

"The Swiss are the same," David said. "Their country is incredibly orderly and clean. You know, I can't believe we're going to have that whole castle to ourselves. Since it's closed two weeks for repairs, no tourists will be able to get in during that time. What a break that Herr Schultz is a friend of the owner and he's letting us go in!"

"Well, I'm glad the workers won't be there today," Penny

said. "Herr Schultz said they were taking a couple of days off, so there won't be anyone to get in our way!"

"Didn't he say there would be a gatekeeper?" Mark asked.

"He did. But the owner called him this morning and told him to let us in. We'll be the only human beings in an entire eleventh-century castle!" David replied.

"We've got to obey all the signs," Penny reminded them. "Some of the rooms and tunnels are not safe, and they're closed to visitors."

"No problem," David answered. "The place is so big that it's got more rooms than we'll have time to explore. That's why the owner said we should bring our flashlights. There's no light in most of the tunnels and rooms."

The road began to climb through the green countryside. Well-kept fields stretched away to either side. Small hills began to dot the landscape to their right, leading to the Taunus Mountains that rose majestically in the distance. They passed through several small villages and finally arrived at Königstein. David parked the car along the street and they got out, taking their sweaters with them. Mark put on his day pack, which contained their flashlights and some snacks.

"How about looking at some of the shops first?" Penny suggested. "Frau Schultz said this little town was a sleepy village until just a few years ago. Then it became a tourist attraction, and now it's got some very expensive shops."

"Well, you don't have a budget for expensive shops," her brother reminded her, "so maybe we'd better give them a clear miss and protect you from coveting!"

"Oh, Mark, you know girls like to look at shops even if

they don't buy anything," she said with a laugh.

David was counting the hotels. "How can this little place have so many hotels?" he asked.

"I told you," Penny said. "It's a real tourist attraction now. Lots of people come here all the time. That's why it's such a treat for us to be able to see that castle all by ourselves."

The narrow street curved sharply, and they saw before them a tower with a narrow gate through it. Obviously, it was part of the remains of the town's ancient fortifications.

"Boy, I'd sure hate to have to fight my way through that!" David said. "How did soldiers get into such places? There's no room! And men can shoot at you from those tower windows and that iron gate."

"You boys stand there and I'll take your picture," Penny said. They stood obediently at the gate under the tower while she adjusted her camera.

"She's supposed to be some kind of a photographer," Mark observed in a voice he meant for Penny to hear. "But see how long it takes her to get a focus? I'd have taken 10 shots in the time it takes her to get one!"

"Yes, but my one picture will win prizes, and your 10 will be good enough to paper the barn with!" she replied.

David laughed. Mark was not that bad a photographer, but Penny was an excellent one. Yet Mark was always teasing her about taking so long to get her pictures.

"Let's go to the castle," Mark said, when she finished.

They turned to their right and began to walk along the curving road toward the ancient fortress. The path became steeper.

"Look at those walls!" David said as they came around a house and saw the towering fortifications on the hill above them. "Anyone trying to capture that castle had to climb over those walls first!"

"Yeah, and to do that they had to charge through volleys of arrows and stones thrown by catapults!" Mark added.

"And arrows from bows and crossbows from the walls above!" David said. "They'd get shot at from every side and from above as well!"

The three wound around the climbing path, then turned right and went up the steep hill. At the top, they found a level spot, a road that led directly to the castle gate.

"Look at all those signs," Penny said pointing. "What do they say, David?"

"This one says 'Do Not Enter!'" David read. And this one says 'Closed for repairs!'"

"Even I can decipher that one!" Mark laughed and pointed to a large sign with one word "VERBOTEN!"

"How about that one?" David pointed. "That says 'Young Americans: Don't Even *Think* of Coming In Here!'"

Penny laughed at David's fib. "I'm getting the feeling they don't want us."

"You're right," David replied. "That is, if you're an ordinary tourist, they don't want you. But you two are not ordinary tourists—you're with *me*. That makes you special guests. So make yourselves at home in our castle!"

"*Your* guests! You mean Herr Schultz's guests," Mark said.

"Well, if I weren't such an expert at the German language,

culture, and history, he wouldn't have dared let you two bumble around in his friend's castle. I'm actually responsible for your privileges!"

Penny laughed at David's outrageous claims as the three approached the gatekeeper's shed on their right. A heavy chain stretched from the small wooden building across the road, blocking the way for cars or trucks.

But when they reached the shed, they found to their astonishment that the doors and windows were closed. David took out his letter of introduction from Herr Schultz and knocked on the door. There was no answer. He knocked again. Still no response.

"This is strange," he said. "Herr Schultz said the guard is always here, and especially now, to keep the tourists out while the castle's being repaired."

"Wonder what's the matter?" Mark asked, a puzzled frown on his friendly face.

"Maybe he went out for coffee," Penny suggested. "After all, those signs and the chain across the road should keep people from going in."

"Maybe," David said doubtfully. He began to walk around the shed. Mark followed him.

"Hey!" Mark said suddenly, pointing to the ground at his feet. "Look at those tire tracks! Someone took off in a hurry!"

The ground had been torn up by tires spinning rapidly. Loose dirt had been thrown for yards along the tracks of the tires.

"You're right," David agreed. "Must have been the gatekeeper. Why would he rush off like that?"

"This is getting more and more strange," Penny observed soberly. "Think we should turn back?"

"No indeed!" Mark said emphatically. "We've got the owner's permission to see this castle, and we've got no reason to be scared off just because the gatekeeper's run away from his post!"

"He probably forgot his lunch," David said with a straight face.

Penny laughed. "You boys just want adventure, that's all. I try to keep you out of trouble, but you won't let me."

"There's no trouble here," Mark insisted. "Just a question or two. Let's go!"

They walked past the gatekeeper's shed and up the path toward the entrance to the inner wall of the castle.

"Here's another wall they had to fight their way over if they wanted to capture this place," David observed. "Man, I'm glad I won't ever have to do that!"

Penny went over to the edge of the green plot of ground and stood beside a low wall. "Look," she said, pointing. "There's the village! I'll take a picture." She began to frame her shot.

Mark stepped close to David. "Let's keep our eyes open," he said. "Something's fishy about this place!"

"It sure is," David agreed. He began to wonder if they shouldn't turn back. But Mark didn't suggest it, so David didn't either.

CHAPTER 5

INSIDE THE CASTLE

The three teenagers walked between the open stone walls to the north side of the castle grounds. Directly below them, steep-roofed houses rose from the village.

"Boy, that's a sheer drop!" Mark exclaimed, leaning over and looking down. A thick hedge grew precariously along the outside of the ancient wall, giving the cold stone fortification a partial cover of green.

They gazed across the tops of houses, past fields and forests, into the distance beyond. Right below them, several small birds fluttered in the shrubbery, seemingly unafraid.

"What a view!" David said. "We can see for miles."

"I want to go into the castle," Mark said.

Turning back, they wandered toward the imposing stone structure. The massive gray wall towered above them as they approached the entrance.

"Why is this tunnel so high?" Penny asked, awed by the height of the stone passageway they were entering.

"They had to have room for men to ride horses in and

out," David replied. "And it had to be wide enough for big supply wagons to bring their food and equipment."

Walking through the entrance of the tunnel, they saw to their right an opening in the stone wall.

"Let's go in there!" Penny said suddenly, her brown eyes shining with excitement. She smiled brightly at David.

"I'll go first," Mark insisted, taking two flashlights from his pack. Handing one to David, he switched on the other and began to follow its beam into the gradually narrowing stone tunnel. A large room opened up to their right as they passed under the castle wall.

"Gosh, this is big!" Mark exclaimed, looking up at the walls in the wide room.

"Maybe they stabled the horses here," David suggested. "They'd want to be close to the gate."

Smaller passages opened off to the sides of this very large space. One of these, more straight than the others, seemed to have a light at the end.

"Let's look in there," Penny said.

"Okay," Mark replied, "but watch your step. This ground is rough."

"And watch your heads," David added. "The ceiling's getting lower."

The dirt floor was uneven, and they moved cautiously. Mark shone his light ahead, scanning both the ground and the ceiling that gradually closed in on them. Penny followed him, and David came next, shining his light ahead of her so she could see where she stepped. The narrow passage made them feel constricted, and each began to remember their adventure in Pharaoh's tomb, where they'd been trapped just a few weeks before.

Finally, they reached the end of the passage where a small window with bars across it looked over a great stretch of land below. Miles away, they could see the dim shape of the Taunus Mountains.

"Boy, what a view!" Penny exclaimed. "I'll take a picture of it that shows those bars." She knelt on the ground and focused her camera.

"I'd get claustrophobia in a hurry if I had to live in this place," David said.

"So would I," Mark agreed.

"Okay," Penny said, closing her camera case. "I got a good picture there."

"Let's look at another tunnel," David suggested.

The three made their way out of the narrow passage. They had all begun to feel trapped under the thousands of tons of stone above them. No one wanted to be the first to mention that, however. Coming back to the larger tunnel, they turned right and continued their exploration of the ancient castle.

Finally, Penny couldn't contain herself any longer. "This sure reminds me of Pharaoh's tomb," she said.

"Me, too!" both boys answered immediately. They'd all felt it.

"Boy," Mark exclaimed, "there were times in that tomb when it seemed like the whole *world* was on top of us!"

"Well, at least we know how to get out of this place," David reminded them. "That's more than we could be sure of in that tomb in Egypt."

"Do you want to go back outside, Penny?" Mark asked.

"Oh, no! As long as I'm with you guys, I want to keep exploring."

"Here's another passage," Mark said, shining his light to the right. "This one's bigger than the last one."

"Let's see what's in it," David said eagerly.

Mark turned and began to lead them into the dark tunnel. Suddenly he stopped, his light aimed at the ground before him.

"That's strange," he said in a puzzled tone.

"What's strange?" Penny asked. She and David crowded behind him and looked at the ground his flashlight illuminated.

"Look at those scrapes in the dirt," Mark replied. "It looks like something's been dragged along the ground."

"Must have been the workers," David suggested. "That's why the castle's been closed—so they could do some repair work."

"Maybe so," Mark said, still puzzled. He lifted his light and flashed it down the passage along the ground, the walls, and the ceiling.

"What was that?" Penny said suddenly, gripping her brother's arm.

"What?" Mark replied.

"Up on the wall, to the right. Shine the light there again."

Mark searched the wall to the right and ahead of them with the beam of his light. Then they all saw what Penny had noticed: a light-colored three- to four-foot scar.

"That's new," David said. "Look how something's scraped the stone."

"Wonder what it was?" Penny asked.

"Whatever it was, it wasn't long ago," Mark added, "otherwise it would be dark like the rest of the walls."

"So, there are scrapes on the ground and a scrape on the wall," David mused. "Somebody dragged something *big* through here. And recently."

"What do you think it was?" Penny asked again, more curious than ever.

They all began to feel a strange foreboding. Yet there was nothing specific to point to, and they couldn't give any reason for the feeling.

"Let's go to the end of this tunnel," David said finally. "Maybe we'll find whatever it was."

"Maybe we'll find *whoever* it was that dragged the thing!" Penny said warningly. "Are you sure we should go on?"

"You bet I am!" David insisted. "This is a mystery and we've got to solve it!"

Mark laughed. "I think you're right. Besides, Penny, there's no danger to us here. This is a tourist attraction—mobs of people come in and out all the time."

"Well, okay," she said. "But let's be ready to get out in a hurry."

The boys agreed. Slowly, the three continued their careful trek through the pitch-black tunnel in single file, following the beams of their flashlights. Then the passage made a sharp turn to the left. Mark flashed his light on the dirt in front of them.

"Look at those footprints," he said.

"They're new," David observed. "Look how sharp and well defined the edges are."

Mark shone his light directly ahead. Against the far wall, a large, bulky mound rose from the floor of the passage.

"What's that?" Mark wondered.

No one answered. The sense of foreboding was even greater. Mark stepped forward cautiously, and the others followed.

"That's a tarpaulin," David said, "and it's covering something."

"Maybe the workers left their equipment here," Mark suggested.

"But this is so far from the rest of the castle," Penny reasoned. "Why would they keep their equipment in such an out-of-the-way tunnel?" She was very suspicious now.

"Let's look," David said. "Here, Penny, hold my light. Mark, give me a hand."

The boys handed their flashlights to her, grabbed the end of the tarp as it lay on the floor, and carefully pulled it away.

"Wow! Look at that!" Mark exclaimed.

"What in the world is it?" Penny asked, mystified.

"A hang glider!" David answered, as awed as Mark. "It's a hang glider! Look how it's been disassembled. See? That's the body and these are the wings."

"What's a hang glider doing in here?" Mark asked in wonder.

"I don't know," David replied, "but look at this wing. It's damaged. The fabric's torn and the tubular frame is bent. They won't be flying anywhere with that wing!"

"But who would be flying hang gliders from the castle?" Penny asked. "This is a tourist attraction."

"Good question," Mark replied. "Maybe the workers fly this in their spare time," he suggested with a grin, not believing it himself.

"Not if their boss knew about it," she insisted.

David looked up sharply. "Do you suppose someone was planning to fly from the castle *without* permission?" he asked. "That might explain why this thing is hidden so far from the main tunnels."

"I bet that's it!" Mark exclaimed. "Someone was doing this without permission, and when he damaged the wing, he had to hide the whole thing until he could fix it."

"Or take it away without being discovered," David suggested. "They might be hiding it here until they have a chance to snatch it away without being seen!"

"I wonder if they bent the wing when they scraped it against the wall back there?" Penny suggested suddenly.

Both boys looked at her intently. "I bet that's what happened," David said. "They damaged it back there trying to get it out and had to bring it back and hide it."

Mark had been rummaging around the other side of the mound, the side still covered by the tarpaulin. "Hey! Look at this!" he said.

David and Penny moved close beside him and followed the moving beam of his light. A dark wire climbed the wall.

"Look at that radio!" Mark said in a hushed tone.

The wire led from the wall into the back of a compact radio set atop a wooden box.

"Gosh!" David said. "What's going on in this place? Hang gliders, radios. What else is here?"

"We'd better get out!" Penny said emphatically. "Someone's got some valuable equipment here and they sure wouldn't want us fooling around with it."

"She's right," Mark said. "Let's put this tarp back the way we found it."

He and David carefully replaced the heavy tarpaulin over the hang glider and the equipment beside it.

"How's that look?" Mark asked.

"Just like it was," David replied. "Let's get out. I want to climb to the top of the tower anyway."

"So do I," Mark agreed.

"Me, too," Penny said.

CHAPTER 6

THE TOP
OF THE TOWER

David led them out, Penny came next, and Mark was last. Carefully they wound their way along the narrow passage, following the beams of their lights.

"I hope no one comes in on us before we get out of this tunnel," Penny said.

The boys had been thinking the same thing. They'd be helplessly trapped if anyone came in now!

Suddenly, something whirred past their heads. "What was that?" Penny cried.

The boys stopped, hearts pounding, and flashed their lights around, trying to find the source of the sound.

"I bet it was a bat," Mark said finally.

"A bat?" she replied. "Oh, I *hate* bats!" She had visions of it suddenly enmeshed in her hair, screaming, clawing to get free.

"It's gone now," David said. "Let's go!"

They moved more quickly now, anxious to get out of this dangerous spot.

"I see light ahead!" David exclaimed. "We're almost there!"

"Let's stop and listen before we go out," Mark said quietly.

They all realized the wisdom of his words. For a long moment they stood still, hearts pounding, listening intently.

"I don't hear anything," Mark said finally.

"Neither do I," Penny agreed.

"Let's go!" David said decisively.

Quickly, they followed him out of the tunnel into the wider passage.

David pointed to his right. "That way!"

They hurried after him, crossing a wide space and moving toward a door cut in the massive stone wall. The sign beside it directed them to the tower steps.

Entering the tower, they began the steep ascent. "Look!" Penny said. "Some of these steps are new!"

"They're repairing it, sure enough," Mark said. "Look at the heavy timbers lying on the platform. Guess they'll replace those old ones."

"Hope they haven't waited too long to do that," David suggested. "We don't want this place to fall down while we're in it!"

"Stop scaring Penny," Mark said with a grin. "You know the owner wouldn't have let us come in if there was any danger of things falling down."

"He's not scaring me," Penny said matter-of-factly. "You've done that all my life, Mark, but I've learned to ignore you!"

"Is that a snake?" David said suddenly, backing into Penny.

Penny screamed. Then as the boys laughed, she pounded

David's shoulder with her fist. "That's not fair! Just when I was trusting you! You're as mean as Mark is!"

"I've been trying to tell you that, but you won't listen," Mark told her.

Face red, Penny told him to be quiet.

"Hold on," David said. "These are real steep now."

He was right. They moved carefully, holding the rail as they climbed, taking their time.

"Look at those iron bolts holding up the stairs." Mark said, pointing.

They saw other pieces of wood and iron lying neatly at the different levels. It was obvious the owner of the castle was taking great pains to make the climb safe for tourists.

"I'm sure glad to see those new platforms and steps!" Penny exclaimed as they climbed. "I wouldn't want to be stepping on the original stairs!"

"Those probably crumbled five hundred years ago," Mark replied.

Penny had a troubling thought: "Do you think those people who own the hang glider will see our footprints when they come back?"

"Probably not," David said. "They won't expect anyone to be snooping around that back passage."

"Besides, we didn't harm anything," Mark added. "What does it matter?"

"It matters if those people are up to no good," Penny said. "I don't think it was workers who put that glider and the radio in the tunnel. It was someone else—someone with something to hide."

David agreed with her. "She's right. That's not a typical thing for repairmen to do. There's another group involved in this, and they're the ones with the glider. And the radio. Wonder why they need a radio for hang gliding?" This thought had been bothering him for some time.

No one had an answer for that. David didn't mention another thought: *What if that other gang returns while the three of us are on top of the tower? What if they find our foot-prints and realize that we've seen the glider and the radio? We'll be trapped on top of the tower with no way to contact anybody or call for help!*

"Here's the top," he said, taking the last step and reaching out to help Penny.

"Finally!" she said, taking his hand gratefully and joining him on the small platform.

"It's a good thing we're in such great shape," Mark said as he stood with them, "or this climb would have worn us out. As it is, David's puffing."

"David's not puffing as hard as *you* are!" Penny corrected him.

The door to the top of the tower was open. Yet for some reason, they did not move.

Penny looked at her brother, then at David. "What's wrong?" she asked.

David realized from Mark's glance that he had been thinking the same thing—they really were alone at the top of this castle tower. There was no one within call. And there was no way out but the way they'd just come. Should that gang come back now and get suspicious . . .

"Nothing's wrong," David said, grinning at her. "Let's go out and see what you can photograph."

"Fine," she replied.

She followed David out of the tower onto a wide stone-floored space surrounded by stone walls chest high. Mark hesitated and looked for a long moment down the stairway they'd just climbed. With a troubled frown, he followed Penny and David onto the outside platform.

"THAT'S HOW THEY DID IT!"

"**W**ow! What a view!" Penny exclaimed, eyes wide with wonder at the vistas before them. The three friends gazed to the south over villages, forests, and fields that strctched for miles to the horizon.

"Those are the Taunus Mountains," David told them, pointing to the south. He unfolded the map Herr Schultz had given him and indicated their present location.

Mark took his binoculars and walked over to the east wall, then the north, gazing at the villages in the distance. Penny followed him, looking through the zoom lens of her single-lens reflex camera, which could serve her as a telescope when she wished. Searching for good photos she focused on houses in the village of Königstein directly below them.

David, still at the south wall of the castle tower, took his compact binoculars out of his pocket and began to search the fields and forests before him.

Penny took several carefully framed pictures, then wandered back to the south wall and stood beside David. The strong breeze blew her light brown hair across her face, and she brushed it away.

"Hi," she said, smiling.

"Hi," he replied, looking directly at her, but with a serious look on his face.

"Why are you frowning at me?" she asked.

"I'm not frowning—I'm thinking."

"Well, you sure look serious when you think. Don't think too often or your face will freeze like that!" she said, with a laugh.

"Don't worry," he replied, grinning. Then he looked serious again. "Penny, I've been wondering . . ." His voice trailed off. He looked directly into her eyes, but she realized that his mind was totally engrossed with something.

"Wondering what?"

He stood for a minute in silence, then turned his head and gazed into the distance toward the mountains. She waited.

What is up? she wondered.

"Look at this map!" he said suddenly, excitement in his voice. He spread it on the wide stone parapet and pointed to the city of Frankfurt. Then he traced his finger along the roads they'd taken to the village of Königstein. "See the way we came?" he asked.

"Yes," she replied, studying the map and following his finger.

"Now, see those towns Herr Schultz marked for us? Königstein—where we are now—and Kappelsberg? And there's Hochheim!" He pointed to the villages their host had marked with red pencil.

Penny nodded, more and more mystified by the growing excitement that gripped him.

"Now, look here! South of the castle. The way we're facing. See this circle he made?" he asked her, his voice intense.

Penny peered at the small, neat letters Herr Schultz had printed on the map. She'd learned already how hard it was to read German handwriting, but these small letters were very clear.

"Villa Braun," she said. Looking into his face so close to hers, she still didn't understand why he was excited.

"Right!" David exclaimed triumphantly. "Villa Braun! Now look to the south through these binoculars and see if you can find that villa." He handed them to her.

"You know I have trouble focusing these small lenses, David," she said, taking them and peering in the direction he pointed.

"The trick is to get your eyes the right distance from them," he said. "Just experiment. Then follow the trail from that road below, across those fields, over the forest, to that hill. It's about two miles away. See it?" he asked, barely able to contain his excitement.

She looked for several moments, searching with the binoculars along the path he'd indicated, finally settling on the villa in the distance.

"Oh, yes!" she said. "I see it!" She looked up. "What about it?" *What in the world has gotten him so excited?*

David took her over to the left where a brass piece with compass directions had been planted on top of the wall. Pointing again to the villa in the distance, he directed her attention to the map.

"Look at the map again, Penny!"

Still puzzled, she studied the map, then looked toward the distant cluster of houses he'd indicated. "I think you're right, David! I think that's Braun's villa! It's just where Herr Schultz marked it on the map! But what about it? I mean, what are you thinking, David?" she asked, putting down the binoculars and looking into his eyes.

He looked at her for a long moment. Finally, he spoke. "I'm thinking about that hang glider in the tunnel below us. And I'm thinking that those thieves who robbed Herr Braun flew into his villa in hang gliders from this castle! His place was supposed to be impregnable, surrounded by a wall with electronic sensors all over it. I'm thinking that some men just sailed over that wall. And that the glider we found below got damaged and couldn't be used. And they hid it there until they could come back and retrieve it!"

He pointed down and to their right. "Look! See that broad wall, the one we stood beside when you took some pictures?"

She nodded.

"Well, they could have run off that wall in their gliders, swung around to their left over those houses, and had a clear sail all the way to Herr Braun's villa! This castle is on a very high hill, and that would give them a real advantage for their flight. Herr Schultz said the news people reported there was no moon that night, so no one would have seen them fly in the dark. Besides, who'd be looking?"

"But the thieves had to have someone inside the villa to cut off the power and shut down the security system," Mark said quietly behind them. They hadn't noticed him walk over.

"Right!" David turned and faced his friend. "They had to have help from the inside!"

Now Mark was as excited as David was. "Herr Schultz said the guests were all unconscious while the place was being robbed and they couldn't tell the police a single detail about it. Well, one or two spies on Herr Braun's staff could have done that! Then they could have gassed themselves to prevent any suspicion! It sure makes sense, David."

"But don't forget," Penny reminded them, "the police said that the system was working when the people woke up and called for help. How could that have happened if everyone was unconscious?"

"That's a good question, Penny," David said. "And the thieves had to think of that, too. I bet the spies who stayed in the villa turned the system back on before they put themselves to sleep."

The more the three talked this over, the more sense it made. Penny interjected a more practical note. "Maybe we'd better get out of the castle before someone comes back. If there really is dirty work going on, and it's connected with this place, we sure don't want anyone to find us here!"

"Boy, that's the truth!" David agreed.

"She's right," Mark said. "We've gotten the pictures you wanted. And we've seen a lot of the castle. Let's get out of here while we're still ahead."

Taking a last look at the marvelous view, they went to the tower door and began to descend the steep steps. Mark led, Penny followed, and David came last.

"Be careful!" Penny warned as they moved cautiously down the narrow wooden steps. She began to wonder if they'd waited too long. Would they encounter the workers, or the thieves, coming up and blocking their escape? What would they do if men appeared and trapped them in the tower?

The descent seemed to take forever. Down they went, around the tight turns at the narrow platforms, then down another set of wooden steps. The stone walls hemmed them in as they descended deeper and deeper into the depths of the tower. Finally, they came to the bottom and gratefully ran out into the courtyard.

"I thought we'd never get out!" Penny exclaimed.

"So did I," Mark agreed.

"Look at those clouds," David said, glancing up at the sky. "The weather sure can change in a hurry around here. Just like Herr Schultz told us. It's getting cold, too."

"Who's hungry?" Mark asked suddenly as they strode rapidly across the enclosed grounds toward the gate.

"I am!" David said. "It's past lunchtime, in fact. Boy, where did the time go?"

"Oh, I'll join you gluttons if you can't wait to eat more food," Penny said with a straight face. "All you think about is eating, it seems. *Someone's* got to keep an eye on you."

"'Can't wait to eat more food'?" Mark asked incredulously. "Penny, it's been hours since we had breakfast!"

"Don't make her eat if she doesn't want to, Mark," David insisted. "She's a real spiritual girl, remember, and doesn't need food like we materialists!"

"Oh, I'll eat to keep you from feeling guilty," Penny said.

None of them mentioned the fact that they were still in danger if the thieves came in the gate before they reached it. They joked as they strode rapidly toward the opening in the high stone wall, praying silently they would get through without being stopped.

Then they were out of the castle grounds. They passed the empty gatekeeper's shed and headed for the path back to the village.

Suddenly, David pointed to their left and suggested they take a shortcut. "Let's go down the hill. It'll save time."

"It's steep," Penny warned.

"We can make it," David said, taking her hand. "Hold on."

They scrambled down the steep bank with Mark right behind them and came out on the path below.

"I've got a funny feeling we should get off this road!" Mark said suddenly.

"Let's go!" David said with a laugh, tugging Penny into a fast run.

She laughed and ran with him, followed by Mark, and the three arrived quickly at the edge of the village. There they slowed their pace to a sedate walk.

"We'd better not call attention to ourselves," Penny warned, "especially since no one's supposed to be going in the castle."

"Then, we'd better hurry and hide in this restaurant," David said.

On their left, right next to the narrow street, was a restaurant with the sign "Gasthaus Zur Traube."

"What does it say, David?" Penny asked. He still held her hand.

"Roughly translated, it means 'At the Sign of the Grape,'" he said. Then he stopped and began to read the rest of the lettering. "Hey, this is old! It was founded in 1471! Let's go in."

CHAPTER 8

SUSPICIOUS MEN AT THE SIGN OF THE GRAPE

A friendly, blond-haired lady greeted them as they walked into the restaurant. David chose a table to the right, by a window that fronted the street. Penny sat with the window behind her, facing into the restaurant, and David sat beside her. Mark sat across the table from them. On the other side of the entrance, to the left of Penny and David, was a small dining room with places set for a private party. In front of Penny and David was a counter that stretched to the back of the restaurant. Several tables and chairs were arranged to the right of the counter, all the way to the back wall.

"I like this!" Penny said, looking around. "And imagine, the restaurant was begun in 1471!"

"Well, this building wasn't," Mark insisted matter-of-factly.

"Of course not," she retorted, "but the restaurant was. That was before the Protestant Reformation!"

"It sure was!" David agreed. He began to read the history of the establishment printed on the menu. Then he read to them the various choices for lunch.

The blond-haired woman returned for their order and David spoke to her in German. Her face brightened, and soon the two were having an animated conversation. David helped Mark and Penny order, then told them that the woman's husband, Herr Brütting, had been private chef to the former president of the German Federal Republic. "Then he retired and they bought this restaurant. He's won all kinds of awards for his cooking!"

Penny studied the red-and-green designs on the chair covers and the brown paneling of the walls. "I think I'll take a picture," she said, uncovering her camera.

David returned to the serious business that faced them. "We'd better plan how to tell Herr Schultz and your dad about the hang glider in the castle," he reminded them, "and how we think those thieves got into Herr Braun's villa." His face was somber.

"Don't forget the radio," Mark added. "That's sure suspicious."

"David's idea really explains how thieves could enter Herr Braun's house," Penny said thoughtfully. "And that damaged glider we saw in the castle seems to be part of the whole scheme."

"But I wonder how the thieves managed to have the castle closed for two weeks so they could launch from there?" Mark asked.

"Some money changed hands, I bet," David replied.

"Well, it wasn't the owner, Herr Schultz's friend, or he wouldn't have let us go in by ourselves and look around," Mark said.

"But who else had the authority to close the castle?" Penny asked. Then her eyes got wide, and she answered her own question: "The manager!"

"Maybe it was," David agreed. "He runs the place for the owner. He had to be the one to give permission to close it for repairs. Who else could let those workers have access?"

"Well, we don't want to be hasty," Mark warned. "It doesn't have to be the manager. Maybe the foreman of the workers is the one who let his men off while the thieves launched their gliders. Maybe he was the one the thieves bribed. We don't want to accuse anyone when we don't really know."

Penny and David agreed. Then Frau Brütting arrived with their plates.

"Let me see the map," Mark said. David handed it over and Mark studied it as he ate. "David, your idea makes more sense the longer I look at this map. Especially since we saw the lay of the land from the tower. You've got to be right!"

Frau Brütting returned as they finished their main course, and she asked if they wanted dessert. David replied, again in German, telling her that they'd like a piece of the chocolate pastry. To his surprise, she answered in flawless English.

"Oh, I've studied English for years," she said, and then smiled. "Lots of Americans and Englanders come to our restaurant, so I get to speak it often. And I've also visited the United States with my daughter. We hope to go next year, in fact."

"That plaque on the wall is about your husband, isn't it?" Penny asked.

"Yes, it is. He was chef for the president before we decided to move to Königstein and manage this restaurant.

Have you seen much of our village today?"

"We've walked around some of the streets," Penny answered, "and we've also explored the castle."

"The castle?" Frau Brütting asked in surprise. "I thought it was closed for repairs."

"It is," Penny answered. Then she told how their friend, Herr Schultz, had gotten permission from the owner for the three of them to see it.

A funny expression came over Frau Brütting's face. She paused a moment, then decided to tell them what she was thinking. "A strange thing happened two nights ago, and we don't know what to think about it. Each day a truck has brought workers to the castle and returned for them in the afternoon. But two nights ago, my husband was taking a late-night walk in the village and he saw that truck leave the castle grounds. It must have returned after dark, then it left again. He was very puzzled by it."

The three teenagers were instantly alert. "What time did he hear the truck leave?" David asked eagerly.

"I don't remember," she replied. "I know it was after ten. We thought this very odd," she repeated. Then she left to get their desserts.

The three were excited now.

"Herr Braun's villa was raided after dark, about nine o'clock, Herr Schultz said!" David reminded them. "That means that the truck left the castle after the raid!"

"They must have gotten a signal that the raid had succeeded," Mark surmised. "Remember the radio we found?"

"It all adds up, doesn't it!" Penny exclaimed.

"It sure does," Mark said.

"But why would they leave the damaged hang glider and the radio and all that equipment behind?" David asked.

They thought about it for a minute. Then Mark made a guess.

"Well, they've got another week before the castle opens up to the public again. Maybe they want to come back when things get quiet. Maybe they didn't want to be on the road with that hang glider in the truck in case they got stopped by the police for something."

"Sure!" David said. "They've got to come back for another week to keep up the appearance of doing the repairs. So they have plenty of time to take away all that stuff. They're just waiting!"

Penny sat back in her chair. "We can't prove this, of course."

"But we sure can prove there's a damaged hang glider in that castle!" David replied.

"With a radio," Mark added.

"*If* the police get to see those things before someone takes them away," Penny insisted.

"Penny's right," Mark said. "We've got to get back and tell Herr Schultz! Those thieves could take away the glider today!"

Before the others could reply, the door opened and two men walked into the restaurant. One was massive, dark-haired, and sullen. The other was medium height with a young-looking face and an almost bald head; what hair he did have was blond. They stood for a moment at the entrance and looked carefully around. They glanced past the three Americans, searching the other tables. Apparently satisfied, they walked to the back of the room and sat down at a table against the wall.

Frau Brütting greeted them, gave each a menu, then returned to the front of the restaurant where the three Americans sat. She handed David the bill.

"Who are those men, Frau Brütting?" Penny asked.

"Those are some of the workers who are repairing the castle," she replied. "They often eat here or come for coffee and pastries." She frowned, then added, "But usually there are more of them. I wonder where the others are?"

"Did you ask them about the truck your husband heard late the other night?" Mark inquired.

"Oh, no!" she said, laughing softly. "My husband reminds me that we've got to mind our own business if we wish to keep our customers!"

David paid for their meals, and Frau Brütting returned to the counter for their change.

"I've got an idea," Penny said suddenly. "I can take their picture. Just in case they're involved in these strange doings at the castle. Maybe that'll help the police."

"Don't let them see you," David warned. "We don't want to attract any attention or make them suspicious."

"Don't worry," she assured him. "Mark, let me focus on the wall behind them while you block me from their view. Then, when David says the men aren't looking this way, lean to your left and I'll get a shot."

"Boy, that's a great scheme!" her brother said admiringly. "Just say when, David." Mark sat facing Penny, his back to the men at the far wall. He formed an effective shield.

Penny focused her camera on the back wall. "Anytime, David," she told him.

David glanced at the men, who were studying their menus. "Shoot now, Penny," he said quietly.

Mark leaned to his left; Penny took two quick pictures and ducked back behind her brother, who returned to his original position.

"I got two good shots!" she said triumphantly, eyes shining.

"Great!" David said approvingly. "You'd make a fine spy!"

Frau Brütting returned just then with their change. After a few words with the friendly lady, the three Americans rose, said good-bye, and left the restaurant.

"Let's get back to the Schultzes and tell them all about this," Mark said.

They walked rapidly toward their car. As David unlocked the vehicle, Mark and Penny looked back the way they'd come.

"See anyone follow us?" Mark asked.

"I don't think so," she replied. "Did you?"

"No. What a break! We got all through that castle and out of the restaurant with pictures of those workers, and no one's spotted us!"

Gratefully, they piled into the car. David drove out of the village and headed back to Frankfurt.

Back at the Sign of the Grape, the two workers were worried.

"Are you sure?" the big man asked his bald friend.

"Very sure," the man replied. "I just glanced in that mirror over the counter when one of those boys leaned to the side. That's when the girl took our picture."

"Let's go!" the big man said decisively.

Slapping down some money on the table, the two men rose at once and hurried out of the restaurant. Frau Brütting was in the kitchen giving their orders to her husband. She never saw them leave.

CHAPTER 9

THE SPIES IN BRAUN'S VILLA

The three Americans had just gotten out of the car and entered the Schultz home when their hostess greeted them with news of an invitation to Joseph Braun's villa.

"We're all invited to spend two nights there. My husband called an hour ago and told me. He and your father have talked with Herr Braun about funding their project, and he says he'd like to. And he wants us all to spend a couple of days at his place while they work out the details."

"That's wonderful!" Penny exclaimed.

"They're already there waiting for us," she added, "so pack for two days and we'll drive there right away."

As they hurried to their rooms, David spoke softly to Mark and Penny. "We'll get to tell your dad what we've found; he can tell us if we should tell Herr Schultz and Herr Braun."

Half an hour later, Frau Schultz was driving them out of the city toward Herr Braun's home. "Are you three tired of all this driving?" she asked.

"No, indeed!" Penny replied. "We're getting to see so

much of Germany. We love it!"

"Well, it's not much longer than the drive you took to Königstein this morning," she said. "We're heading south of the castle you visited."

She asked about their trip and they told her, but they didn't mention the damaged hang glider or their suspicions. The drive took them through countryside as interesting as what they'd seen in the morning. Sometimes Penny would snap a picture through the car window.

An hour and a half later, Frau Schultz turned the car into a well-paved lane and headed toward the estate of Joseph Braun. Broad fields stretched to either side of the road, and she began to tell them of his large farming operations. Topping a rise, they saw Herr Braun's villa perched on a hill ahead of them, surrounded by a long stone wall.

Frau Schultz stopped the car at the gatehouse. A powerfully built man in gray slacks and shirt came to the car, checking the license plate with a card he held in his hand.

"Herr Braun is expecting you and your friends, Frau Schultz," he said. "Drive right up to the house and park in the front beside the other cars."

As they drove through the gate, the Americans noted another gray-clad man in the guardhouse built into the wall that surrounded the villa.

"This place really looks secure," Mark commented.

"It looks secure," David replied, "but someone got in."

"They did indeed," Frau Schultz added.

"Did you notice the video camera above the guard's window photographing us as we drove through?" Penny asked.

No one else had noticed it.

As Frau Schultz spoke to Penny, Mark said in a low voice to David, "I'm convinced that your idea is right. How else could anyone have gotten in this place? Those hang gliders *have* to be the key!"

The curving lane took them past a large garden before leading them to the house. Frau Schultz parked beside her husband's car and she and the trio started toward the front door. Before they reached it, Herr Schultz, Jim Daring, and Herr and Frau Braun emerged to greet them.

That night, after an elaborate meal enlivened by wonderful tales of the Brauns' travels abroad, the three teenagers walked with the adults onto the terrace. They had not yet had a chance to speak to Mr. Daring about the castle and were getting nervous, wondering when they could tell their story. The Brauns began to discuss the robbery.

"The police suspect that the thieves may still be hiding close to here," Herr Braun told them. "When that drunken driver hit the van they were in, the crash knocked it off the road. The thieves escaped on foot carrying a fortune in jewels with them and may still be in the neighborhood."

"But haven't the police combed the forests and surrounding fields, Joseph?" Herr Schultz asked.

"They have," their host replied, "and they haven't found anyone yet."

"Where are they looking now, Herr Braun?" Mr. Daring asked.

"Well, of course, the thieves couldn't have gotten back into the villa," Herr Braun replied, "so they're searching for them outside the walls, in the area surrounding the spot where they went off the road. They're covering the countryside."

"Didn't the thieves also take one of your trucks?" Herr Schultz asked him.

"They did," Herr Braun admitted. "And we wonder if they've kidnapped some of my security force, because two of them are missing."

The teenagers wandered to the right, off the edge of the patio and around the side of the elaborate house. The sun was setting behind the hills to the west, and its rays flashed across the lovely countryside, throwing the grounds into shadow.

"Which way is the castle from here?" Penny asked as they strolled.

"That way." David stopped and pointed to the north, pulling his compact binoculars out of his pocket. Focusing them, he studied the high hill that still basked in the sunlight. "That's it!" he said.

"Looks like it'd be an easy glide from that hill to this one," Mark observed. "It's much higher than we are here." Mark turned, his face frowning in concentration. "I've been thinking. The police are searching the countryside outside Herr Braun's walls. They're assuming the thieves tried to get as far away as they could from the scene of the crime."

"Isn't that logical?" his sister asked.

"Sure it is," he replied. "But what if it's wrong? These thieves are smart! They've done the unexpected already in gliding over the walls. What if they did the unexpected and came back here? Back where no one's looking for them?"

"That's a good point," David agreed. "They know everyone

will expect them to get as far away as they can. Maybe they did the opposite." His face lit up with the possibilities.

"But they couldn't come back without help, could they?" Penny asked. "You saw the security at the gate."

"You're right," Mark agreed. "They couldn't come back without help."

"But that's what we've already decided they had to have to get into the villa in the first place," David said. "They had to have spies planted among Herr Braun's people to shut down the security system, to put everyone to sleep with that gas, and to let them out the gate with the vehicles and turn on the system again."

"Then the same spies could have helped the thieves get back in and hide here where no one's looking for them. Is that what you're thinking, Mark?" Penny asked.

"Well, it makes sense, doesn't it?" he asked in reply.

"It sure does," David agreed. "I never thought of that!"

"Neither did I until a minute ago," Mark admitted, and grinned. "But it suddenly occurred to me that someone smart enough to pull off this theft must be smart enough to do the unexpected when they got into trouble getting away. Dad always told me how important it is in war, or in a fight, to do what the other guy doesn't expect you to do!"

"And no one seems to think they'd try to get back inside the walls of the villa," Penny agreed. She thought for a moment. "You know, if you're right, they'll have to lie low for a while before they can get away."

"We'd better tell your dad right away!" David said urgently.

"And tell him why we think this theft was an inside job, too," she said.

Mark added a sobering thought. "If what we suspect is true, and Herr Braun's own people are in on this robbery, then we can't be too careful ourselves. I mean, we don't want to attract any suspicion or talk about this where we might be overheard. We don't have any way of knowing which of the people working in the house are spies."

That was a serious thought indeed, and David and Penny pondered it as the three began to walk back to the patio where they'd left the adults. They *had* to tell Mr. Daring about this! As they approached the patio, they saw that Mr. Daring and the Schultzes were seated, still talking with the Brauns.

"How can we talk to Daddy?" Penny asked Mark anxiously.

"We'll have to wait a while longer," Mark replied.

"Let's keep walking around the other side of the house, then," David suggested. "We haven't seen the view from that side."

"There's not much to see in the dark," Penny replied.

"You're wrong, Penny," Mark said. "Look at the sky! We're seeing stars we can't see in Africa!" Mark was an amateur astronomer, and he delighted in the new constellations they were able to view in the more northern latitudes of Europe.

Suddenly he stopped. "I'll be right back!" he said. "I'm going to get my binoculars."

David and Penny continued walking slowly as the light faded and more stars appeared. "Oh, David, I wish we could talk with Daddy about all this!" she said.

"So do I," he replied. "But we'll have to wait until he's through talking with the Brauns. We *think* we're right about how the thieves got in this place, but we don't really *know*, and we don't want to make foolish statements. Your dad can tell us what he thinks of our ideas."

They walked slowly along the garden path. Their eyes were becoming more and more accustomed to the dark now, and they began to recognize more constellations. "There's Orion!" Penny said. "He's huge!"

"He sure is," David agreed. "And he's got a bunch of interesting stars and star clusters. The Greeks and the Romans called him 'The Hunter' and said that the three stars slanting down from his belt represented his sword."

Mark rejoined them then. They were now some distance from the house, and the darkness was almost complete. It was so dark, in fact, that they could just make out a low stone wall ahead of them two feet above the ground, surrounding a small garden. Sitting on this, they continued to gaze at the stars in contented silence. Mark looked through his binoculars. David held Penny's hand, and she rested her head on his shoulder.

Suddenly she straightened. "Look!" she whispered to David.

"Where?" he whispered back.

"Over there, to the left! In the woods!" She pointed.

David could barely see her arm. Peering intently toward the woods, he saw nothing but the dark smudge of the forest. The line of trees was about 100 yards from the house, but it was so dark that nothing could be seen within them.

Then he saw a light flash! Twice, three times, then twice again.

"I saw it!" he whispered. Reaching out his right hand, he touched Mark's shoulder. "Quiet! There's a light from the woods!"

Mark was instantly alert. "Where?" he whispered.

Before they could reply, a foot scraped on stone just a short distance to their left. They froze! Mark turned his binoculars slowly in that direction and searched for a moment.

He leaned toward David and whispered, "There's a man standing there. I can see him through my binoculars."

At that moment, they saw the man flash a narrow beam of light at the ground in front of him, just for a second, to see his way. Then the light was switched off. Mark continued to watch the mysterious figure as he moved quietly and carefully down the gentle slope toward the woods.

David whispered to Penny, then to Mark, "Don't move. There may be others nearby."

None of them moved or spoke for five minutes at least.

Finally, Mark whispered to David, "He's reached the woods! And I don't see anyone else around here. I've searched with these glasses." The wide lenses of the binoculars gathered so much more light in the dark than did their eyes—that's how Mark could see the man walk to the forest.

They huddled their heads close together. "I bet those are some of the spies," Penny said.

"And thieves," David added.

"Let's try to mark this place in our minds," David suggested. "Mark, study the woods for any break in the tree line that might help us spot where the man went in. We can come back in the morning."

Mark peered intently through the binoculars. "I can find the exact place," he said confidently.

"Maybe we can take a walk tomorrow," David said, "and see what's down there."

"We might find more than we want to find," Penny said. "I don't think that's a good idea at all!"

"Well, we can walk around the grounds at least," he answered. "Something might turn up to explain what those men are doing."

"Sure," Mark added. "We can ask the Brauns if we can take a walk in the woods. Bring your camera, Penny, so you can take pictures all the way. No one will suspect anything if we do that!"

"That's right!" David said eagerly. "We can wander around in no particular direction, so it won't seem as if we're aiming for the spot where the men went in. Then when we get inside the woods, we can turn and head over that way. Maybe we'll find something that'll explain this mystery," he concluded hopefully.

"First, we've got to talk with Daddy!" Penny insisted.

"You are absolutely right, Penny," Mark agreed. "Let's go find him. There shouldn't be anyone around now."

As the three walked back to the patio to seek Jim Daring, Penny had a sudden feeling they were walking into terrible danger.

CHAPTER 10

THE EXPLORERS

When they returned to the terrace, they found Mr. Daring and the two German couples in the process of saying goodnight. The three teenagers joined the adults, thanked the Brauns again for their hospitality, and walked back with Mr. Daring to their rooms. Penny was staying in a room near her dad; Mark and David had a room of their own.

"Daddy, we've got to talk to you and Herr Schultz!" Penny whispered as she walked beside her father down the hall. "Can you ask him to come to your room?"

"Sure, honey," he replied, puzzled at her earnestness. He let the teenagers go ahead while he dropped back and asked Carl Schultz to join them for a minute.

"Be right there, Jim," Herr Schultz replied.

In a few minutes, Herr Schultz joined them in the room. Penny and her father sat on one of the beds, Mark sat in a chair against the wall, and David stood.

"Thanks for coming, Carl," Mr. Daring said as he waved him to the remaining chair. "These folks say they've seen something suspicious." He turned to Penny.

"Well," she said hesitantly, "we ought to start at the beginning. And David figured it out. Tell them, David."

"Okay," he agreed. He told of their drive to Königstein and their visit to the castle. Then he told of the damaged hang glider hidden with some radio gear under a tarpaulin in one of the castle's tunnels. He described the view from the tower and the clear path a glider would have sailing from the castle to Herr Braun's villa.

"They could glide over fields almost all the way," Mark interjected, "and no one would have noticed them!"

"If anyone had thought to look up," Penny added. "And even if he had, it was so dark they wouldn't have seen anything. There was no moon that night."

David then told of their suspicions about a spy being in Herr Braun's villa. "Someone had to turn off the security system so the gliders could get in the yard without setting off the alarms," he said.

"The police thought of that, too," Herr Schultz interjected.

"And someone inside had to turn the gas on all the people to put them to sleep when the robbers came in!" David continued.

"We think it took several people to do that, Dad," Mark said earnestly, leaning forward as he spoke, "because they had to gas the rooms with the guests as well as those with the servants and the security people."

Penny took up the tale. "Then, just a little while ago, we were outside in the yard looking at the stars, and we saw a light flashing from the woods! A minute later, we heard someone near us in the dark. We'd been quiet so long that I guess he hadn't heard us. He flashed a light back at the person who'd signaled him, then he began to go down the hill toward the forest."

"I followed him through the binoculars, Dad!" Mark said. "Those wide lenses gather a lot of light, and I could see him all the way to the woods. He went to join whoever had been flashing that light."

When the teenagers finished their story, Mr. Daring and Carl Schultz looked somberly at each other for a long moment without saying anything. Herr Schultz was the first to speak.

"All this is very suspicious, Jim," he said finally. "I know Joseph Braun will want to hear this."

"I think so, Carl!" Mr. Daring replied. He thought a minute. "But he's on his way to bed now and I hate to interrupt him. Let's tell him first thing in the morning."

Herr Schultz agreed to this, and after a few more words the group broke up. Herr Schultz returned to his room.

Mark, David, and Penny prepared to go to theirs as well, but something in Mr. Daring's manner stopped them. He was standing with a thoughtful expression on his face, obviously pondering his next words to the three teenagers. Finally, he spoke.

"See that small black box on the floor by the bed?" he asked, pointing. They looked and saw the object he indicated. "On the side is a red switch. Flip that, Herr Braun told me, and a signal for emergency help flashes to the nearest police station. Only two of the guest rooms have this—Herr Braun has it, too, of course—and he wanted me to know about it.

This system is battery-powered, so it doesn't depend on the electrical power that runs the rest of the house."

He stood thoughtfully a moment longer, then grinned at the three. "But I know you won't have any need for that knowledge! Let's read the next chapter in Exodus, then go to bed. Tomorrow we'll tell Joseph Braun just what you three saw in the castle today. And what you saw outside the house just now."

Mark read from Exodus, then each of them prayed. When they finished, the teenagers went to their own rooms. It had been a long day for them, and they fell asleep at once.

The next morning they learned that Herr Braun had received an urgent call and had already left the villa.

"He'll be back by supper," his wife told her guests. "He asked me to apologize for him, but this is connected with the robbery. He had to meet with the police." Her kindly face showed concern that her husband had to leave his guests.

"We understand," Mr. Daring replied.

"But this won't interrupt our plans for the day," Frau Braun hastened to add. "I'd still like to take you on a tour of our property."

After breakfast they all went with her to the front door where a van was waiting. For two hours, they drove around the large estate while Frau Braun described the various workings of the farm. At the barn, a farmhand let Mark and David drive a tractor. When they returned, the teenagers asked if they could walk around and take pictures.

"Certainly!" Frau Braun replied. "Help yourselves. If you want to go through the gate, the guards know you, and

I've told them to let you through."

"Why not take something to eat and drink with you?" Mr. Daring asked them. That was the policy they had always followed, and it had come in handy in the past.

"I'll have our cook prepare something for you," Frau Braun volunteered instantly.

"Thank you, Frau Braun," Penny said gratefully.

Their hostess left to give the cook instructions.

"Just keep your eyes open," Mr. Daring said to the three.

"We will, Dad," Mark assured him.

"Jim, let's use this time to go over our plans for your project in Egypt," Carl Schultz suggested. "I think we can finish this in a couple of hours."

"Excellent, Carl!" Mr. Daring replied. "Let me get my briefcase and we can meet on the patio."

In a short while, Mark, Penny, and David were walking down the hill away from the house. Mark had put the lunch the cook had prepared into his day pack, which he'd slung over his shoulders.

As soon as they left the house and started walking down the hill, Mark began to explain the course he'd plotted. "That light we saw last night was just about southwest of the house. I think we should head directly south and go in the woods, then cut to our right and look for the place where we saw the man signaling. We don't want the spies in the house to get suspicious, and they sure would if they saw us heading straight for the place they're using!"

"Good idea," David agreed.

The three wandered in a leisurely manner southward from

the house, veering to the left and right as they saw things that interested them. Periodically, they stopped while Penny framed pictures. Several times she turned back and pretended to photograph the house. Actually, she was studying it carefully through her zoom lens to see if anyone had been watching them.

"She's quite a weapon in our arsenal!" Mark observed quietly to David as they stood a few feet away and watched her.

"That's the truth!" his friend agreed. "Nobody looking this way would realize that she's really scouting with a powerful lens!"

"I don't see anyone watching us," she said as she rejoined the boys. "At least not outside. But we really couldn't see anyone standing in one of the rooms."

Nevertheless, they were encouraged that they didn't seem to be noticed as they moved closer and closer to the woods.

"If we think anyone's watching us," Penny said thoughtfully, "we can always walk over to the gate and go out in the fields."

"That might be a good idea," Mark agreed. "But first let's see what we can find on this side of the wall. Someone was signaling from under those trees, so there's got to be something there—some sign or trail, or *something!*"

They reached the edge of the woods and stopped. At once it was cooler. The trees towered above them now and shaded them from the sun. Standing for a moment in this peaceful place, they looked around. Birds sang from within the woods.

"Everything's so restful," Penny observed.

"Let's hope it stays that way," David said.

"Look!" she said, suddenly pointing into the trees ahead. "What a pretty bird!"

"Let's go," Mark replied. "In case anyone's watching, we're just innocent explorers."

Laughing, the three walked under the trees and into the woods. David led, Penny followed, and Mark brought up the rear. The bushes were thick and close together, and they were forced to go in single file. Quiet now and alert, the three glanced repeatedly left and right as they moved deeper into the dark woods.

After they'd gone about 30 yards, David turned and looked back. "We're out of sight of the house!" he said.

"Let's not get lost!" Penny warned.

"Don't worry." David grinned, showing her his pocket compass. "We won't."

"We'd better go a little farther, David," Mark suggested, "just to make sure no one can spot our clothes through any break in the trees."

"Right," David agreed. "Let's go." He led them another twenty yards or so, then stopped. "I think we can turn right now—that's to the west—and see if we can intercept the trail those people made last night."

Standing in the deep, shadowed woods where no wind penetrated, they all began to feel the heat.

"Let's go slowly so we don't trip on anything," David said.

"And quietly," Mark added. "If there are others nearby, we want to hear them before they hear us!"

Suddenly they realized that what they were doing might actually be dangerous.

Penny voiced their thoughts. "You know, if we really are near the people who stole those jewels, we don't dare let them see us!"

For a moment, David wondered if they should return to the villa. "No one back at the house knows where we are, do they?" he asked, a frown on his face.

"No, they don't," Mark agreed. "But Frau Braun and her staff know we're wandering around the yard, so I can't see that we're in any danger."

Still, none of them moved. "Well," David said finally, "if we do run into anyone, let's just act friendly, like tourists, and keep going. Penny, keep your camera handy so you can pretend to take pictures."

"Okay," she said. The camera was in its case, hanging from her neck. She could quickly and easily open it up.

With a sense of foreboding, they turned to their right. Following the needle of his compass, David led as the three stalked quietly through the thickening bushes. It was dark, but there was enough light filtering through the branches of the trees above to let them see their way.

Penny suddenly noticed that the birds had stopped singing. All they could hear was the faint sounds of their footfalls on the ground.

What will we find? she wondered, and she shivered.

CHAPTER 11

"WHERE'S DAVID?"

Slowly and carefully, the three teenagers wound their way through the thick brush and around the trees. The woods were silent, ominously so . . . almost threatening. To Penny, the trees seemed to be actually closing in on them, leaning down and blocking the way ahead, closing off their retreat. It was an eerie feeling. She shuddered.

"You okay?" Mark whispered from just behind her.

"I guess so," she whispered back. "It just seems so . . . threatening!"

"It does to me, too," he agreed. "But I don't think it really is. We're just guests here, and Frau Braun invited us to explore the grounds. So we're not doing anything wrong."

"But those people who stole the jewels did do something wrong," she replied. "And if they find us snooping too close, they might be dangerous!"

Mark said nothing. He had begun to think the same thing. Maybe they should turn back and get out of these woods right away!

Just then David stopped and held up a warning hand. Quietly, they came up behind him.

Holding a finger to his lips, he leaned close to them and whispered, "I thought I heard voices."

They stood still as statues, hardly daring to breathe, straining to hear the voices David had heard.

After several moments, Mark became restless. "I don't hear anything," he whispered.

"I don't either now," David agreed. "Maybe I was wrong."

"I don't think it's worth taking a chance," Penny said quietly, her brown eyes troubled. "Why don't we go back?"

Neither Mark nor David replied. They hated to give up, especially when they had no real reason to quit.

Finally, David said, "I don't hear anything. Let's go on."

"I agree," Mark said. "Want me to lead for a while?"

"Not yet," David replied. "But I've got an idea. Just in case we do run into anyone, you two drop back about 10 yards. Or as far as you can and still see me through these bushes. That way, if I run into anybody, you can listen and see if it's safe to keep coming."

"What if it isn't safe?" Penny asked, alarmed at the idea of David walking into danger.

"Well, in that case, you two can start back, and I'll come back, too."

"What if you run into people who won't let you come back?" she insisted.

"Then you two go back anyway and get help. I'll be all right."

"No!" Mark said decisively. "If we go quietly enough,

you'll hear anyone before he sees you. If it doesn't look safe, you just turn back right away and we'll all retreat."

"Okay," David agreed. "Let's go."

"I don't like this at all," Penny whispered, but David was already ahead and didn't hear her. She turned back to her brother. "Mark, I don't like this!"

"Well, I really think everything's okay. After all, we're actually in Herr Braun's yard, and the guards at the gates keep out anyone who shouldn't be here."

"But what about those men flashing lights at each other last night?"

"Hurry, Penny! Don't let David get out of sight!"

Frantically, she turned and started after David, heart pounding, wondering if he'd gone out of her vision already.

But then she saw the back of his shirt briefly through some branches. Hurrying carefully, she moved ahead and soon was able to see him easily. Just then Mark caught up with her.

"Let me pass, Penny," he said quietly. "I'll go ahead. You stick close."

She let him by, then came close behind.

The ground sloped downward suddenly and Mark almost fell. Regaining his balance, he turned and pointed down to warn Penny to watch her step. She smiled nervously and stumbled over a fallen branch. He reached out quickly and held her arm in his strong grip.

"Careful," he said reassuringly.

"Thanks," she said, regaining her balance. He steadied her for a moment.

When they resumed walking, David was nowhere in sight.

Mark started to rush forward, then stopped suddenly. It was no time to forget caution. Turning, he whispered to Penny, "I can't see David!"

"Where could he be?" she asked, frightened.

Back at the villa, Jim Daring and Carl Schultz sat on the patio, working over their papers. Frau Braun had gone to the nearby town right after the teenagers left, and the two men had gotten a lot of work done.

A servant came out to the patio and handed Herr Schultz a note. "Herr Braun just called and asked us to give you this message, sir."

Herr Schultz thanked the man, opened the envelope, and read the note. He beamed. "Good news, Jim! The police have found some evidence that seems very promising. Joseph invites us to join him at the police office in town. The chauffeur will take us there."

"That's splendid!" Mr. Daring said. "But I hate to leave without the kids."

"They're picnicking on the grounds, inside the wall, sir," the servant assured him. "We saw them just a few moments ago." He paused, then continued: "The chauffeur is waiting for you at the front door."

"Well, in that case . . . ," Mr. Daring paused, still hesitating.

"I'll be happy to go to them right away, Mr. Daring," the servant said quickly, "and tell them you and Herr Schultz are going out for a short while."

"Well, thanks," Mr. Daring said. Then he made up his mind. "I'm sure they're okay in this place."

"Especially since they're within the walled area," Herr Schultz agreed.

"Let's go, then," Mr. Daring said decisively.

The servant smiled slightly as the two men entered the house and headed for the front door. Looking after them, he waited for sounds of the car's engine. Then he turned and walked quickly down the hill toward the woods. His orders were urgent: They *had* to find that girl and take her camera and all her film! She'd taken pictures of their men at Königstein, and the gang couldn't let the photos fall into the hands of the police.

CHAPTER 12

TRAPPED!

Mark stood in desperate thought. He couldn't let his friend David face danger alone. But he couldn't take his sister into peril. What should he do?

"Mark," Penny whispered frantically, tugging at his arm, "we've got to find him! He must be just ahead!"

"I'm not sure what to do, Penny," he whispered back.

"But we have to find him!" she insisted. "What if he's hurt?"

"I can't take you into danger," he said firmly. "We've got to be sure you're safe. Then I can find David."

Just then they heard a crashing noise ahead of them.

"Shhh!" Mark warned.

Standing in silence, they listened to the sound of heavy footsteps fading through the woods.

"Who could that be?" she whispered, frantic with fear for David.

"I don't know," Mark replied, "but it's more than one man. Be quiet!"

Not daring to move a muscle, they listened until they could hear no more.

"Mark, someone must have captured David! We've got to find him! Oh, please!" She had tears in her eyes.

"Maybe we can," he said hesitantly. "I sure can't leave you now, not with men all over the woods! Let's stay off the trail and follow the way David went. We've got to be quiet. But maybe we'll catch up with him. I bet he's hiding, just like we did when we heard those men."

They walked cautiously in the direction they'd last seen David, the same direction toward which the footsteps had just gone.

Suddenly, they heard voices to their right heading toward them!

"Quick, Penny!" Mark whispered urgently. "Crawl under those bushes!"

She dropped to her knees and crawled several yards into the thick brush. He followed her. She stopped at the base of a large tree and turned as Mark joined her. The two huddled together, hidden behind thick brush.

The voices came closer.

"They're speaking German!" she whispered.

"If only David were with us!" Mark said.

Then it seemed that the heavy footsteps were heading toward the spot where they'd last seen David.

"Mark!" she whispered suddenly. "I think I can see through the bushes!" Quickly, she unstrapped her camera and aimed it through the leaves. She thought she'd seen a clear spot. "I'll use the telephoto lens," she told him with growing excitement.

"Don't move, though!" he warned. "People can see movement, but lots of times they can't see you if you're still."

"I won't move," she replied. "Look there, Mark. That's where I think they'll pass." She pointed.

Mark leaned to his left and looked through the leaves toward the clear spot she indicated. Three men passed by in single file speaking words the two Americans could not understand. But then Mark's heart leaped with gladness as he saw that two of the men wore gray shirts. "Look! Those are the security guards! They'll help us find David!" He started to rise.

"Wait, Mark!" she whispered, grabbing his arm. "That man leading them is the worker I photographed in the restaurant!"

"What?" he asked. "What worker?"

"The bald man in the restaurant in Königstein. Remember? Just after we came out of the castle. Frau Brütting told us that the two men who came in while we were eating were workers at the castle. I just saw one of them!"

Shocked, Mark sank back to his knees.

"But what does that mean?" he asked. "Why would one of the workers at the castle be here?"

"I don't know."

"Penny, are you sure?"

Crouching in the dense undergrowth, they faced the implications of this news: A worker at the castle, who'd worked unusually late the night of the robbery, was walking with Herr Braun's security guards!

"I'm *sure*!" Penny insisted. "I know I saw that man in the restaurant while we were eating there. He's got a young face, but his head is almost bald. I took his picture. You know I remember faces, Mark! That's one of the men Frau Brütting said worked at the castle. I *know* he's one of them!"

Mark had learned long ago to trust Penny's knack for observation, so he didn't make a move to call the men.

The footsteps faded, and the two teenagers sat in anguished indecision.

"Penny, that means the workers at the castle are in cahoots with Herr Braun's security guards! This proves David is right. Guards inside the villa had to be working with the thieves who came in from the castle!"

"And if the thieves really did launch their gliders from the castle," she said, "then those workers had to be part of their gang. That's how they could use the castle! It was closed to visitors, so they could launch from there!"

They knew they were right.

"But, Mark," Penny said, "how can we help David?"

"Maybe I can follow those men," he suggested hopefully. "If you stay here, I'll see if I can find out where they've gone. And where David hid. He must have seen something and hidden himself," he said emphatically. "You know he didn't blunder into anything."

Suddenly, more men came from the path to their right, following those who'd already gone the way David had pursued.

"Shhh!" Mark whispered, holding Penny's arm.

They didn't dare move. But suddenly the footsteps stopped!

Penny's heart leaped! What had alarmed those men? With wide eyes, she looked up at Mark.

"Penny, start crawling that way," he whispered. "We've

got to get away. But don't make a sound!"

He pointed to his left, directly away from the men. Silently, she began to crawl. Mark followed just as quietly.

Then they heard voices! The men were leaving the trail and heading this way, and they were speaking German! Neither Mark nor Penny understood the language. How they both wished David were with them!

"Penny, they're following us! Hurry! But be careful," Mark whispered.

They continued their crawl through the woods, frantic now, but not daring to panic. They knew that a single sound would confirm the suspicions of their pursuers.

"Left, Penny!" Mark whispered as he saw a thicker patch of bushes to that side.

Obediently, she turned to her left. Carefully, Mark looked at the tall trees before him. He had to keep a careful bead on landmarks or they'd be hopelessly lost.

Behind them, the silence was alarming. Mark continued to crawl behind his sister. Wisely Penny chose a path under the thick clump of bushes, thus putting the natural barriers of the woods between them and the men who might follow.

Suddenly, she came to a stone wall. "Oh, Mark! We're trapped!"

CHAPTER 13

NO WAY TO TURN!

The sudden cry of a bird had drawn David's eyes away from the path for just a moment, but in that moment he'd stepped into a vertical tunnel.

Stifling a cry, he plunged downward, barely catching the edge of the square frame surrounding the hole. Desperately, he gripped the frame as his feet groped for the rungs of the ladder he'd glimpsed in his fall.

Finally planting both feet on the ladder, he held on and caught his breath. Climbing swiftly up the rungs, he scrambled over the edge to the ground above. Then he saw the square hatch cover of the tunnel lying in the bushes to his left. He knelt on the ground, praying that no one had heard the sound of his body slamming into the wall of the vertical tunnel.

Suddenly, David heard footsteps and men's voices approaching from the direction he'd just come . . . where Mark and Penny should be! His eyes searched frantically for a hiding place, but there just wasn't enough cover within reach. *I've got to go down that tunnel and hope they don't follow me!* he thought.

Quickly, David crawled over the edge and began to go down the ladder, his rubber-soled shoes making no sound as he rapidly descended into darkness.

When his feet touched the floor of the tunnel, David guessed it was about 15 feet below ground. Looking to the left and right, he saw no light in either direction. *I've got to get away from this ladder!* he thought, knowing that he could be seen by anyone who stood directly above him. But which way should he go?

Making a quick decision, he moved to his left, walking carefully, feeling his way along the wall with outstretched hands. The tunnel was no more than five feet wide, and he could touch both walls as he walked.

His heart pounded, and he struggled to keep his mind clear as he moved into the darkness. The light from the tunnel entrance behind him grew dim. If there was anything on the ground before him to make him stumble and fall, he sure wouldn't be able to see it in time!

I was a fool not to bring along that Mini-Mag-Lite, David thought. He'd relied on Mark having one in his pack, but Mark wasn't here! *That's a lesson Dad taught me over and over,* he said to himself bitterly.

David moved more slowly as the darkness ahead became total. As he walked, he prayed that he wouldn't bump into something that would trip him up. He was in a tomb, buried underground, separated from Mark and Penny, heading he knew not where.

Maybe I should stop here while I can still see the light.

Turning, he faced the distant light that still filtered down from the forest above. It seemed like a tiny smudge of faintness in a sea of black ink.

If no one comes down that ladder, I can wait a while, then go back and climb up, he thought. The only alternative was to continue walking into the blackness. Maybe those men he'd heard were gone; maybe he could go back up the ladder!

David began to retrace his steps carefully. He'd rejoin Mark and Penny, and they'd go back to Herr Braun's house at once!

He'd taken only a few steps toward the ladder when the distant light was blotted out. The sound of men's voices came from the opening above. Someone was coming down!

Frantically, David turned and began walking away from the ladder, holding his hands against the walls on each side, blindly groping his way. Every step he took was a risk—he could crash into anything! But he couldn't delay. Surely those men would have flashlights!

Their voices filled the tunnel behind him. Turning back for a desperate glance, David saw the bright beams of a powerful light bouncing down the tunnel. Fortunately, it was aimed at the ground, not at him. But the men were moving quickly. And they were coming toward him!

He was trapped unless he could find a hiding place before they caught up with him. But how could he move in the darkness as fast as they could walk behind their light?

Above ground, at the wall that encircled Herr Braun's villa, Mark and Penny faced a desperate choice.

"Which way shall we go?" Penny asked in an anguished

whisper. "They're closing in on us!"

"Let's go to the left!" Mark said. "That way, we're at least heading toward the gate."

Penny walked quickly through the vegetation that seemed to fill this part of Herr Braun's property. Mark followed closely as she weaved around thick clumps of bushes and under tree branches heavy with leaves. Behind them, the sounds of approaching steps grew closer.

Penny looked anxiously over her shoulder and whispered to Mark, "They've almost caught up!"

"Maybe not," he said hopefully. "We're heading away from their path. Maybe they'll stop at the wall!"

And it seemed that they did. As Mark and Penny continued to walk away from the spot where they'd found the wall, the sound of the men's steps and voices began to fade. Then it sounded as if they were going back the way they'd come.

"I think they stopped at the wall and then went back," Mark whispered to Penny as he walked closely behind her. "But keep going. We've got to get a long lead in case they follow us."

They continued their stealthy escape, perhaps 30 more yards. Then Mark put his hand on Penny's shoulder.

"Let's think a minute," he said.

Penny stopped. Her face was so worried that Mark put his strong arm around her. She leaned her head on his chest and closed her eyes.

"We'd better go back to the place we last saw David," he said quietly. "Maybe he had to hide in a hurry just like we did. We've got to steer a course to intercept the trail we've made."

"But, Mark, you know he would have turned back to warn us if he'd seen any danger. He never would have just hidden himself. Something stopped him from coming back."

"I know," Mark admitted. But for the life of him he couldn't imagine what it was. David would never have let them walk into danger without alerting them; he'd risk his life to do that.

Penny began to cry quietly. Mark put his other arm around her.

"Let's go find him," he said. "But this won't be easy, because he's got the compass. We've got to find the landmarks ahead, then look back and make sure we're going in a straight line. You're good at observing things, Penny. You'll have to help me."

Wiping her eyes with her sleeve, she nodded. He took her hand, looked at the wall, then fixed his gaze on a tall tree some 15 yards away, about 45 degrees from the path they'd just followed along the wall.

"Let's head for that tree," he said. "When we get there, we'll find another in the same direction and go to that. We'll just go for one tree at a time. That way we can be sure we're heading roughly in a straight line."

They began to make their way toward the tree they'd picked as a landmark. When they reached it, they found another and did the same thing, always trying to stay in a straight line away from the place they'd started. Sometimes Mark had to let go of Penny's hand so they could proceed in single file, but as often as he could he took her hand in his and walked beside her. It was slow going, but it was steady and sure as they went back toward the spot where they'd last seen David.

After a while, Penny stopped. "I recognize that tree! We passed it when we followed David!"

"Good!" Mark said. He wasn't sure about it, but he knew how she remembered what she saw, and he trusted her. "Let's turn left then and go that way."

They turned and continued their careful trek through the bushes. Mark also recognized the path they'd been on earlier when David was with them.

"This is it, Penny!" he said exultantly. "You were right. We did it! We intercepted the path we were on with David. Thank the Lord!"

"Oh, Mark!" she said. "What could have happened to him?"

"I don't know," he replied. "But I bet something forced him to duck in a hurry before he could warn us. I bet he knew we'd spot danger when he disappeared, and I bet he counted on us to hide. And that's just what we did." Mark tried to sound optimistic.

The forest was silent. Shadows thrown by the sunlight falling through the tall trees made ominous patterns on the bushes and the ground. Penny shivered and squeezed her brother's hand.

"We've got to be careful," Mark warned. "We're not far from the place where we lost David."

More slowly now, they crept along, straining to be silent, listening intently for any sound of David . . . or danger.

Penny thought they'd been creeping along for an hour, though she knew it hadn't taken that long. Suddenly, Mark stopped. Turning, he put his finger to his lips. For several moments, they stood frozen, listening with all the concentration they could muster.

What alarmed Mark? Penny wondered. *Is it so close that he can't even whisper?*

CHAPTER 14

CAUGHT UNDERGROUND!

In total blackness, David felt his way along the narrow passage, seeking desperately to escape the men coming swiftly behind him. Reaching out his hands, he ran them along the walls as far ahead of his body as he could, hoping his fingers would touch a door before he slammed his body into it.

Suddenly, his hand did feel a door! Instantly, he stopped, groping in front of his face as he felt a smooth surface. *Metal!* he thought. *What kind of tunnel is this? Is this part of Herr Braun's security system? Or does he even know about it? Did his men who had been in league with the thieves make this tunnel without Herr Braun's knowledge to enable them to steal from him at will?*

David felt for a handle, found it, and prayed, "Oh Lord, please let this be unlocked!" Slowly, he turned the knob and pushed. The door opened! Stepping quickly through, he closed it behind him and began to grope his way forward again.

The tunnel grew wider. Suddenly, David could no longer feel the wall on his left. What should he do? Those men were right behind him. But if this was a room, and they switched on a light, he'd be discovered!

He moved along the wall to his right, one hand grazing the wall, the other groping ahead of him, praying there was nothing on the floor to trip him up. Then he heard the voices of the men in the tunnel. They were speaking German, and they were at the door!

Frantically, David moved along the wall. Suddenly, his hand felt only air! Taking several steps, he found he was in a small alcove. Then his hand found a ladder on the wall.

Just as the men opened the door, David began to climb up the ladder. Then the door slammed and someone flipped a switch, flooding the room with light.

But David was out of their sight, crouched on a platform above. As the men moved into the room, he froze.

"Those kids came down from the villa and just disappeared!" one of the men said in German.

"Olaf told us the girl is the one who photographed them in the restaurant near the castle! We've got to get her and her camera!"

"Well, they can't get out the gate. Siegfried will grab them if they show up there. They've got to be somewhere in the forest," the other man replied.

"But where? Karl just told us that Daring and Schultz were lured out of the villa by a false message, and that he came straight here to warn us that those kids were exploring the woods. But we haven't seen them. How can three kids just disappear?"

A door opened and a harsh voice said brutally, "They

can't! Find them or we're all in jail!"

"But Kurt, we're searching the woods! Five of us have been looking for them. And they've just dropped out of sight!"

"Find them before they find us!" Kurt replied.

David heard Kurt move into the room below him as he continued to give orders. "We can't have the police suspect that we ran this way when the van was hit. If they search these woods inside the walls of the villa, we're sunk. We've got to find those kids and get rid of them before they can bring the police down on us!"

"All we have to do is capture one of them," one of the men replied. "Daring wouldn't let Braun call the police if one of his kids was in our hands. Just grab one of them and use 'em as a hostage until we can get out of here with the jewels."

David's heart leaped! So that was what had happened! The thieves had run back toward the villa when their van was wrecked, back to the place the police would never suspect, back to the scene of the crime! And the jewels were somewhere close!

David crouched on a narrow platform at the top of the ladder he'd climbed so desperately. The small platform was shadowed by the light that came from the room below so that he could barely see ahead of him. He seemed to be in some kind of storage space—boxes of various sizes were stacked around him. Afraid to make any sound, hardly daring to breathe, he kept absolutely still.

Kurt—whoever he was—had his way. The two men agreed to go back above ground and renew the search for the three teenagers. David heard the door shut. Still he waited, not daring to move. Then the light in the room was switched off, and he heard the other door close, the one Kurt had come through. Plunged into blackness again, David, his heart pounding, continued to wait, wondering what to do. The men who had come down the tunnel behind him were on their way to search for Mark and Penny. Other men were above ground also looking for them.

What chance do Penny and Mark have of escaping those searching men? he thought. *And how many of Herr Braun's servants are in cahoots with the thieves? How many of his men are in on this robbery? Who can be trusted?*

Then another thought struck him: *This could be my only chance to get out of the tunnel!* Maybe he could follow those two men out of the tunnel and above ground. If they planned to go into the woods to join the others in the search, he'd have a chance to get away. But he'd have to be careful; he couldn't follow too closely or he'd be caught.

Slowly—carefully trying not to knock into anything in the blackness—David let himself down the ladder to the floor. Then, with his left hand on the wall, he moved painstakingly toward the door through which he'd entered just a short while before.

Touching the wall to his left, David crept through the darkness. It seemed to take an eternity, but finally he was at the door.

His great fear was that Kurt might suddenly come into the room behind him and switch on the light.

David's heart thudded in his chest as he slowly gripped the handle and eased the door open. Far down the pitch-black tunnel, he could see the light of the men's flashlights on the floor as they hurried toward the ladder.

Closing the door quietly behind him, David moved quickly along the passage. The men's voices were faint now; he thought he saw them blot out the light from above as they climbed out of the tunnel.

If they change their minds and come back down, I'll be trapped! he thought as he continued his rapid pace toward the ladder. But it was his only choice; there was nothing else to do. He had to get above ground and help Mark and Penny get away from the men who were searching for them. He couldn't let them be captured and used as hostages!

The light coming down through the square opening was getting stronger. Soon David saw the outline of the ladder against the wall. Slowing his pace, he strained to hear the voices of the men he was following.

But David heard nothing. Maybe the men were standing above the tunnel listening for their friends, trying to decide which way to go to join the search. He knew he had to be careful now. After coming this far, he didn't want to make a foolish move and be captured. Slowly he crept closer to the ladder.

Still David heard no sound. Reaching the edge of the patch of light, he stopped and looked up. Standing motionless, he listened and waited in indecision. *How long should I give those guys before I climb up this ladder?* He'd be utterly helpless if he came out while they were still standing there.

Suddenly, he heard Penny scream.

CHAPTER 15

"RUN, PENNY!"

Several minutes before David reached the ladder, Mark had been leading Penny toward the place they'd last seen their friend. Stopping suddenly, he whispered, "I hear voices ahead!"

"Oh, Mark, what should we do?"

"I don't know, Penny." He knew only that he first had to get her out of danger and he then had to get his dad and Herr Braun to start a search for David.

But which way to go? Back at the wall that enclosed Herr Braun's villa were at least two men—they'd barely eluded them by cutting to the left and returning another way. But just ahead, toward the spot where David had disappeared, other men were talking. Were these Herr Braun's loyal servants? Or were they the companions of the man Penny had photographed in the restaurant, the worker at the castle?

Mark made up his mind. "Penny, we've got to get out of these woods and into the open. At least some of Herr Braun's servants are loyal, and if just one of them sees us, people will know where we are."

"Okay," she agreed, her brown eyes filled with anxiety. "But I hate to run away from David."

"So do I," Mark agreed. "But it's our only chance to get away, and if he's in trouble, we're his only chance of getting help. We've got to get out of these woods!"

Taking Penny's hand, Mark turned to his right and began moving quietly through the thick bushes clustered around the trees. Suddenly, he stopped and turned toward his sister.

"Penny, I'll go ahead," he whispered. "You follow a few yards back. If I run into something, you sneak around us, then run for the villa."

She nodded silently, her heart sinking. *How will I get away if people capture Mark? Won't they capture me at the same time?* But she knew it was the best plan they had for getting through the woods. She let Mark get a short lead, then began to follow.

Mark felt encouraged. They were heading toward the house, at least, and would soon be out of the woods. He turned and winked at Penny to cheer her up. She smiled back tremulously.

Mark never saw the vine that tripped him. One moment he was walking carefully through the bushes, the next he was crashing to the ground! Leaping up, he faced three men as startled as he was—the two gray-clad security guards and the bald worker from the castle.

They charged him. Penny screamed.

"Run, Penny!" Mark yelled.

Turning to his right as if to run away, Mark planted his

right foot, lifted his left knee, and jabbed his foot into the stomach of the nearest guard. The man crumpled to the ground. Whipping around to his right again, Mark planted his left foot and slammed the other guard in the chest with his right heel. A rib cracked, and the man staggered backward and fell.

Without saying a word, the worker from the castle smoothly pulled a pistol from his jacket, aimed it at Mark's chest, and cocked the hammer.

Mark stiffened instantly, not daring to move. The man jerked the barrel upward. Mark raised both hands above his head.

The man glanced quickly at his two downed companions. Both were writhing on the ground and gasping for breath, obviously out of action for a while. Cursing viciously, the bald man jerked his gun at Mark, waving him back toward the entrance to the tunnel. Mark started walking, and his captor followed warily a few yards behind, the gun aimed at Mark's back.

Meanwhile, David had bolted from the tunnel and stood for a moment, desperately searching for Penny. Below ground there'd been no way he could tell from which direction the scream had come. But now he heard the commotion in the woods to his left, toward the villa. He started that way, then stopped. Someone was coming toward him!

Which way to go? In terrible indecision, David stood for a moment. *I've got to get out of sight!* Moving carefully to his right, he melted into the bushes, crouched behind a thick screen of branches, and peered through the leaves.

Barely five yards away, Mark and the castle worker passed

by, heading for the tunnel David had just left. Sick at heart, wondering where Penny was, David watched them disappear. *Can I jump that man with the gun and rescue Mark?* he thought.

Then he heard moaning. Quickly, he moved through the bushes and trees until he came to the spot where the injured men writhed on the ground.

Mark must have put those guys there! David thought. *But where is Penny?* Anguished, he stood there, wondering what to do. *Maybe she got away. Mark wouldn't have quit fighting unless she had . . . or unless they both had been captured by the gunman.*

Yet, Penny was nowhere to be seen. *Should I search for her? She must have gotten away!* David thought. *That's the only thing that makes sense.*

Just to make sure, David made a quick search, moving in a widening circle around the spot where the injured men lay. Then he saw a trail of sorts—crushed branches leading in the direction of the villa. *Someone in a hurry broke those branches*, he concluded. *They weren't worried about making noise! Penny must have gotten away! She'll go to the house and call the police!*

David stood for a moment. *I've got to follow Mark and see if I can help him!* Turning, he moved swiftly but quietly toward the tunnel entrance.

Barely an hour ago, the three had left Herr Braun's villa together. Now each was alone and in danger.

A hundred yards away from David, Penny burst through the edge of the woods and ran toward the house. She gripped her camera bag in her hand, eyes searching to the left and right, desperately seeking one of Herr Braun's servants so they could call the police for help.

But how will I know whom I can trust? The awful thought grew in her mind that she had no way of knowing who was loyal to Herr Braun and who was not.

Penny was in great physical condition, but the uphill slope and the awful fear began to sap her strength as she ran. Breathing deeply, she continued her pace toward the house. Finally, she slowed to a walk.

I can't let myself be captured by one of those spies! But how could she avoid that, since she had no idea which servants to trust? *I'll stay outside until I get a couple of them to call the police*, she decided. That way she wouldn't be captured and locked in a room.

Penny remembered the kitchen: Several cooks and maids were there! They couldn't all be spies! She'd go around the house to the kitchen and call through the window for someone to come out. Then she'd explain the disappearance of David and the capture of Mark and have the kitchen help call the police. Pleased with this plan, she veered to her left, intending to go around the building.

As she approached the patio and prepared to walk around to the kitchen, two men came out of the house. Looking intently to their left, neither of them had seen her. Instantly, Penny dropped to the ground out of their sight. Noticing a shallow trench just ahead of her, she crawled toward it.

Her mind was in turmoil. *How can I reach the people in the kitchen with those men standing guard?*

Another thought struck fear in her heart: *Can I be seen from the woods?* She glanced back anxiously. The shallow trench was deep enough to hide her from sight. But she was trapped there—she couldn't go forward because of the men, and she couldn't go back because of the danger in the woods.

David had been captured—she and Mark were sure of that. Mark hadn't followed her, so he must have been captured, too. She had to get to the kitchen and call the police! But as long as those men stood there on the patio, she was trapped in that shallow trench. And she didn't dare raise her head to look at them.

Mark, meanwhile, found himself descending a ladder just ahead of the man with the gun. At the bottom he stopped but quickly moved a few steps into the tunnel when his captor, halfway down, gave a harsh command and waved his pistol. Then the man switched on a flashlight and shoved Mark in the back. Mark began walking along the narrow tunnel, wondering where he was being taken. And wondering if Penny had reached the house yet. And wondering where David was. *Have they captured him, too?*

Finally, Mark came to a door. "Enter!" the man behind him said in English. Mark opened the door and stepped through. His captor followed. Inside, the bald man switched off his flashlight and turned on the light in the room. Mark had no way of knowing that David had been in that same room just a few minutes before.

Again his captor shoved him forward. Mark moved ahead, walking quickly toward the door opposite him. He guessed that was what the man wanted. Glancing to the left and right, he saw boxes piled in neat rows. *Wonder what's stored in those?* he thought.

"Enter!" the man said again.

Mark opened the door and stepped into a room. Two men sat in chairs to his left, but they leaped to their feet and drew pistols when he walked in. Shocked, Mark halted. The man behind him shoved him forward violently and began to talk to the two men in a torrent of German. Mark couldn't understand a word.

CHAPTER 16

ESCAPE INTO DANGER

David stood behind a tree some yards from the tunnel entrance, not daring to go after Mark and his captor right away for fear of being taken himself.

Maybe I'd better give them a couple of minutes. I know there are two guys down there—the bald one and the one called Kurt, who ordered those others to search for us.

Just how David would be able to jump two armed men in the tunnel, he didn't know. He just knew he couldn't leave Mark in their hands. *Maybe Kurt will be in another room*, he thought hopefully.

In less than five minutes, he heard men rushing through the tunnel just 10 yards away. Then they scrambled up the ladder, one after the other. David shrank behind a thick clump of bushes and burrowed deeper into the branches. He could barely make out the men's faces as they emerged from the tunnel, but he recognized the bald man and a security guard. The bald man was speaking angrily in German.

"We've got to get to the treasure and meet that helicopter!

Our men in the house will lock up the staff! I called off the search for those kids—they don't matter now! What matters is getting those jewels and making our escape from this place!"

"How far can we go in a helicopter without being tracked by the police?" the guard asked.

"It's got hospital markings!" the bald man replied. "People will think it's a rescue craft. We'll take it 100 miles west to a narrow road, then drop down in the woods and transfer to the truck. By the time Braun returns, we'll be a long way away. He won't have any idea what happened, and his people won't be able to tell him." He laughed, and the guard laughed with him.

"What a haul!" the guard said admiringly. "This will bring millions!" The men moved away and their voices faded.

David knew it was the time to go down the tunnel for Mark. He got up and moved quickly toward the entrance. The men had put the square door on the opening. David lifted it easily and set it aside, then went down the ladder. He hurried along the way he'd already been, touching the walls on each side to keep his bearings.

Then he began to hold his left hand ahead of him while he guided himself along the wall with his right—he didn't want to crash face first into that door!

There it was! He paused and listened for sounds from within but heard nothing. The darkness was complete. He felt like he was back in Pharaoh's tomb—only there, he and Penny had had light sticks to illuminate their way. David turned the doorknob carefully and eased open the door. The room was in total blackness as it had been the first time he entered. He groped for the light switch until he found it, then flipped it on and prepared to fight anyone inside.

There was nothing in the room but the boxes he'd seen before. Quickly, he crossed to the far wall and faced that door, the one through which Kurt had entered.

Is there anyone guarding Mark? Have they hurt him? David knew he'd have to be ready to fight anyone inside, but from what Kurt had said, he knew the guards were probably on their way to the house. He switched off the light in the room and slowly turned the door handle. Opening the door, he stepped into the room and felt for the light switch. Flipping it on, he swept the room with a glance, body balanced.

Mark sat in a chair to David's left, hands taped behind him, feet taped to the chair's legs. There was no one else in sight!

"They're gone," Mark said quietly, his eyes wide at the sudden appearance of his friend. "I don't know where they've gone, but I have a feeling they've left this tunnel for good. Let's get out of here!"

"I know where they've gone," said David. "I'll explain as soon as we're out of this tunnel." David whipped out his pocket-knife and sliced the tape that held Mark's hands and feet.

Mark stood up and began to rub circulation into his arms. "Where did you come from?" he exclaimed. "We thought they'd captured you! You just disappeared in front of us!"

"I fell into this tunnel," David replied. "When I started to climb back out, I heard men coming, so I ran down that hall and found a loft in the other room. I had just reached it when two men came in. They almost got me."

"Well, they *did* get me!" Mark replied.

"But where's Penny?" David asked anxiously.

"She ran to the house to get help! She'll get them to call the police!"

"Not if they catch her first, she won't!" David said. "We've got to get back and help her. There's no telling how many of Herr Braun's men are really working for these thieves! And they're searching the woods for us!"

"But they've got guns," Mark answered, his blue eyes troubled. "That's how they got me."

"Did they leave any guns here?" David asked quickly.

Both boys began to search the place. Both had a high respect for guns. They had been trained in their use since they were young boys and knew the importance of being careful with them. David hurried to a set of drawers against the wall, while Mark opened a trunk on the floor.

"They sure did!" Mark exclaimed. He pulled out several holstered pistols and handed one to David. The boys carefully removed the guns from their holsters and examined them.

"Take some extra clips!" Mark said.

Stuffing an extra clip in their pockets, the boys ran to the door. David grabbed the handle, then paused. "Let's turn out this light," he warned, "just in case someone's come into the next room."

Mark switched off the light and the room was instantly drowned in darkness. Carefully, David opened the door with his left hand.

The other room was dark. Gratefully, he felt for the switch on the wall and flipped it on. They rushed across to the other entrance. Mark again switched off the light, and David carefully opened the door to the tunnel.

That, too, was absolutely dark.

"Thank the Lord!" David said gratefully. "Let's go! Put your left hand on the wall and follow me!"

In complete darkness, the two boys rushed down the hall.

"How will we get to the house without being seen?" Mark whispered as they hurried carefully through the darkness.

"I don't know!" David admitted. "Maybe we can go through the woods to our left and come to the back of the villa."

"That's a longer way," Mark observed.

"I know it is. But maybe we'll have a better chance of avoiding those men," David replied.

As fast as they could, the boys pressed through the total blackness of the tunnel, wondering if it would ever end. Finally, they saw the growing patch of light ahead of them.

"There's the entrance and the ladder!" David said excitedly. "We'd better slow down."

Carefully, they moved toward the ladder. The bright light from above illuminated the floor ahead of them.

"I'll go up first," David said.

Before Mark could protest, David began to climb. His heart was pounding. *What if there are guards waiting for us above ground?*

At the top of the ladder, David cautiously raised his head and looked around. "There's no one here!" he whispered "Let's go!"

Scrambling out quickly, David began searching the woods as Mark came out and joined him. David told Mark what he had heard the bald man say about getting the jewels to the helicopter. So the thieves probably wouldn't be at the house.

"We'd still better go another way," Mark said. "Let's head left and go toward the edge of the woods. We'll end up nearer the back of the house."

"Fine," David agreed.

The two moved rapidly through the woods, slanting left but heading toward the villa.

"I've been praying that Penny's safe," Mark said.

"So have I," David said.

Both of them had never been separated from her before—not when there was danger—and they realized they'd failed somehow.

"David, I *had* to send her away when those men charged us!" Mark said. He felt anguish at the thought of his sister fleeing alone.

"You sure did!" David agreed. "And that's how she got away. Don't second-guess yourself, Mark. There was nothing else you could do. Your job was to fight and let her escape. And that's what you did."

They raced through the woods as fast as they could, running where possible, anxious not to make too much noise, but thinking there were probably no men around to notice.

Up on the hillside, not far from the house, Penny wrestled with the options before her. *I can't go back to the woods, but I can't go straight to the house. I've got to work my way around to the kitchen!* She began to crawl along the narrow trench that paralleled the hillside. It seemed to head toward the back of the villa, so she kept moving.

Periodically, she glanced at the woods. The trench was just deep enough to keep her from seeing all but the tops of trees. *That means no one can see me!* Neither could she see the house. She was thankful for that, because that meant the men on the patio couldn't see her either.

Painfully, she worked her way along the narrow trench, crawling slowly, keeping her body as low as possible. The rocks were cutting her knees and hands, but there was nothing else to do. She pressed on.

Once she heard men's voices to her right, from the house. She froze, heart pounding, thinking they'd spotted her. But after a moment of waiting, she heard nothing else. No one appeared. Carefully she began to crawl again.

Penny was sweating as she struggled in the heat of the sun. No breeze reached her in the narrow depression along which she moved. Realizing that she hadn't been keeping careful watch to each side, she began to glance left and right, making sure she was not in view of anyone. But no one appeared in her vision.

She had to rest. Dropping flat, she rested her head on her arms and prayed. It seemed so hopeless now. Probably David was captured. Mark no doubt was a prisoner. She didn't know where her father, Herr Schultz, and Herr Braun were. Men allied to the thieves roamed the house and the woods, searching for her, Mark, and David.

Penny remembered Israel's king. He, too, had crawled desperately through the hills and wilderness of Judah, barely escaping the soldiers of vengeful King Saul. *But the Lord rescued David*, she thought, *and He can rescue me, too.* She began to recite the Twenty-third Psalm.

Determinedly, Penny started to crawl again. Her knees and hands were bleeding, but she couldn't stop. She *had* to call the police so David and Mark could be rescued from those men!

It seemed like an hour had passed when next she stopped. She'd heard shouting from behind her and to the right. Had she gone far enough? Maybe she was near the kitchen! Slowly, she raised her head and looked toward the house.

Two men ran from the side of the house and out of sight. Ducking her head in fright, Penny waited several minutes. Then she lifted her head again and searched to left and right. There was no one in view.

Penny continued crawling along the narrow trench. *This must be a drainage ditch*, she thought. Dimly, she remembered Frau Braun telling her about this. It had come in handy today! Glancing again to the right, Penny saw the roof of the house. Finally, she was near the kitchen. Rising carefully, she searched the building.

She didn't see anyone.

Something's wrong! she thought. There had always been action around the back of the house—people coming and going from the gardens, as well as from the vans in which they did their shopping. The place had been bustling that morning. What had happened?

CHAPTER 17

"THEY'RE GETTING AWAY!"

Deep in the woods, Kurt and the bald man struggled with the two injured guards, the men Mark had disabled. One stumbled along still clutching his stomach; the other limped badly, favoring his injured rib. Helping the men through the woods had exasperated Kurt and his companion. After joining the two, Kurt had immediately sent the guard back to meet the men with the jewels. Now he was impatient with the injured men and their slow pace.

"Get a move on!" Kurt snapped viciously. "The helicopter's almost here! If we don't show up, it'll leave, and we'll spend the rest of our lives in jail!"

But the injured men could move no faster. Helped by the bald man and Kurt, they limped painfully and slowly toward the edge of the trees. Ahead of them, the others had gathered the stolen loot and stood waiting at the tree line for the helicopter. Two of Herr Braun's guards and one of the thieves who'd arrived by hang glider stood just inside the trees. Beside them on the ground were narrow cases containing a fortune in jewels stolen from Anatole Navarre. The two other hang glider pilots had gotten away in the truck that had escaped the night of the robbery. Kurt and the remaining man had been in the van that had overturned in the accident on the road.

"Lucky for us we were close enough to Braun's estate to bring these cases of jewels to the gate," the glider pilot said to one of the guards.

"And lucky for you we were on duty and let you in the gate while everyone at the house was still asleep from the gas!" his companion replied with a grin. "We sure didn't expect to see you come back!"

"We didn't expect to come back, but we had no choice. When that drunken fool knocked our van off the road, we were lucky to be close to the gate and to the tunnel where we could store these gems and hide ourselves from the police."

"There are two of those tunnels in these grounds," the guard observed thoughtfully. "We use them for bunkhouses and for storage; that's so one attack can't knock out all the guards at once—at least that's what Braun thought when he designed this place. They each have two entrances from the ground above."

Just then he spotted the four men struggling through the woods to join them. "Here they come now," he observed. "And here comes the helicopter. Those guys just made it!"

Excitedly, the men scrambled to gather the containers with their fortune in jewels. The roar of the chopper's engine began to pound their ears.

At the villa, Penny had just reached the kitchen door. She heard no one. The place was quiet as a tomb. Heart pounding, she opened the door and peeked inside. No one in sight! Stepping quietly inside, she looked around fearfully. Still she saw no one. *Where are the cooks, the butlers, and the maids— all the people who filled the bustling room before?*

Then she saw the telephone hanging on the wall directly across from the door. Quietly, she rushed across the floor and picked up the receiver. There was no dial tone! For a moment, she knew real despair.

They've cut the wires or something, Penny thought, almost panicking. *Now no one can call for the police! There's no way to reach anyone for help!*

Suddenly, she remembered the little black box beside the bed in her father's room. It had an emergency signal that reached the police! And it was powered by batteries that didn't depend on the villa's generators!

I've got to get to that room! she thought desperately. But where was everybody? They must have been captured and locked up. Would she be able to reach the room?

Penny tiptoed to the hall door, which was ajar, and carefully stepped through. As she walked quietly toward the bedroom wing of the house where she, her father, and the boys were staying, each step brought greater fear, for each brought her closer to possible danger.

Any moment she expected to see a gray-clothed guard or a household servant walk out of a room. But the house was silent. Absolutely silent. Once Penny bumped into a chair standing next to the wall. Instantly, she froze, expecting a guard to rush out and capture her. But no one came.

Resuming her careful trek toward the bedroom wing,

Penny came to the wide opening that intersected this part of the building. Halls led to the left and to the right. Her father's room was to the right. Peeking fearfully around the corner, she saw no one.

The thick red carpet muffled the sound of her footsteps. The dark paneled walls hung with marvelous works of art decorated her fearful passage. The dread of discovery was almost overpowering. Penny prayed for courage as she moved tremulously toward her father's room. She was so close.

Finally, she reached the door. Gripping the knob, she prayed that God would protect her. Carefully turning the handle, she stepped inside, her heart leaping with joy. She'd made it! Now she could use that signal and call the police!

The dark-suited man standing at the window whipped around at her entrance and stared at her bleakly.

Meanwhile, at the bottom of the hill, Mark and David halted at the edge of the woods.

"We'd better scout the area before we leave these trees!" Mark warned.

David agreed. Together they searched the hillside, looking carefully toward the villa, then to the left and to the right.

"I don't see anyone," David said.

"Neither do I," Mark replied.

Both boys were sweating from their rush through the thick woods. They stopped to catch their breath. Standing together, they had almost decided to start ascending the hill toward the villa when they heard the sound of the helicopter.

"Back!" David urged, stepping deeper into the woods. Mark did the same.

The sleek, white-painted helicopter with hospital markings swooped low across the field from left to right, passed the spot where the teenagers were standing, then hovered 40 yards away before settling to the ground. It faced directly away from them.

"That was close!" Mark exclaimed in awe. "Half a minute more and I was going to suggest we run for the house! We'd have been caught in the open with no way to escape!"

David looked soberly at his friend. "I was thinking the same thing."

They could see through the bushes that several men were moving toward the chopper, two of them being helped by others.

"Are those the men you kicked?" David asked.

"That's them!" Mark replied.

David grinned at his friend. "You sure took a chance attacking them when the other man had a gun!"

"He didn't pull that gun until those men were on the ground," Mark replied. "I know not to fight men with guns in their hands!"

"Well, you threw a monkey wrench into their plans to search for us," David said. "They had to quit so they could grab the jewels and get those men to the chopper. You saved Penny from capture, Mark!" David looked long at his friend and thanked the Lord for his courage.

"Look!" Mark said suddenly, pointing at the men who'd rushed from the woods to the helicopter.

David looked where his friend was pointing. Three men were bringing long cases in their arms and handing them to the men inside. They returned to the woods several times for more cases. Then Kurt and the bald man came in sight and spoke briefly with two of the men in the gray uniforms of Herr Braun's security crew. These men nodded, turned, and faded into the woods.

"I bet they're pretending to be loyal guards!" Mark said bitterly. "How many of them are really working with those crooks?"

"No telling!" David answered. "But Herr Braun has really been fooled by the men he trusted. Looks like half of them are spies! No wonder they could release that gas in all the rooms and put everyone to sleep when they robbed the place. Then they let the thieves enter the gate of the villa with the jewels after their van was wrecked. They must have helped collect the stolen stuff and carry it to the underground tunnel, because those glider pilots couldn't have done it all by themselves!"

"Looks like they're going to get away after all," Mark said.

"Wait!" David said suddenly. "See those external tanks on both sides of the helicopter? What if we shot those when they took off? Nobody could hear our guns when that engine's going full power."

Mark thought about the idea before replying. "I bet we could do it," he said finally. "It's certainly in range."

Both boys looked intently at the two tanks on the lower side of the helicopter, then drew their guns from the holsters.

"With the helicopter facing away from us, the angle's perfect!" David observed. "Get ready! We'll fire when they rev up the engine and get in as many shots as we can. You take the right tank and I'll take the left!"

The men had closed the door of the helicopter. The engine was roaring, the rotors were whirring, and the craft was about to take off!

Both boys moved closer to the edge of the woods, lay on the ground, propped their automatic pistols, and took careful aim. The helicopter's engines went to full power, and the craft began to lift. David and Mark began to fire deliberately.

The machine rose from the ground with a tremendous noise. The boys stopped firing and ducked their heads as the chopper's blades blew dust and small stones along the ground and over their bodies. The helicopter tilted forward, then swooped out of their sight over the trees, the sound of its engines beginning to fade. The gray-clad guards were nowhere in sight.

"We'd better be quiet and look out for those men," Mark whispered.

"Okay," David agreed.

They turned to their right and faced into the woods searching the bushes and trees with their eyes, looking for anyone who might attack.

CHAPTER 18

TRAPPED IN THE VILLA!

Ten minutes earlier, Penny had entered her father's room to hit the switch that would call the police. Now she froze, camera case in her hand, staring at the strange man who stood by the window, blocking her way to the emergency switch by the bed.

The man stared at her without speaking for a long moment. Finally, he broke the silence.

"Are you one of the Americans who are visiting the Brauns?" His accent was thick but his speech precise.

"Yes," she replied, heart pounding. To reach that signal box, she had to go to the wall where the man was standing. Apparently, he'd been looking out the window and now he was between her and the box. How could she call the police? Who was this man? What would he do?

"Thank God!" he smiled. "There's been another robbery! Some of the security guards locked everyone in the basement. I just happened to be outside and came in just as they were doing this. Fortunately, they didn't see me. But they've sabotaged the phone lines, and I can't call the police!"

"I can!" Penny answered. Walking quickly toward him, she turned and went to the head of the bed. She stooped and flipped the red switch on the small black box. Her heart was pounding as she rose and turned to face him. Is he telling the truth? No matter now; the police had already received the signal and they'd be here soon!

"That calls the police," she said.

"Good!" the man said with relief as he sank into a chair by the wall.

Then Penny knew he was a friend. For the first time in a long while she began to relax.

"I'm Penny Daring."

"I'm Fritz Horning," the man replied, "an insurance agent for the Brauns. I'd just driven up to the house, but I came to the wrong entrance. That's how I missed being captured with the others. I saw the guards force them all downstairs."

"Where did the guards go then?" she asked quickly.

"They went outside on the patio. They never looked for anyone else. Then they headed down the hill. I ran for every phone I could find, but none would work. Then I headed to the basement to release those people they'd captured, but I thought I heard someone enter the house, so I ran down the hall and hid in this room."

"I saw those two guards," she said. "But I hid in a narrow trench and crawled around to the back of the house."

"How long will it take the police to come?" the man asked.

"I don't know, but Herr Braun is a very important man.

He told my father that they'd get here in a hurry if he ever had to use that emergency call." Then she thought about the noise Herr Horning had heard, the noise that had caused him to hide in her room. "But who did you hear after those two guards left?" she asked, alarmed.

"Maybe it was you," he suggested with a smile. "I heard a door shut in the back of the house."

Penny grinned in relief; it *had* to have been her. She'd made the noise that had sent him scurrying to hide!

Penny's mind flew to the plight of David and her brother. *What happened to David? How could he disappear so suddenly in front of us? And what happened to Mark after he attacked those men so I could escape?* She began to cry.

Miles away from the villa, in a speeding helicopter that swooped low over fields and farmhouses, jubilation reigned. The men inside were whooping and hollering at their successful escape.

"We're finally out of that tunnel!" Kurt shouted above the noise of the engine. "I thought I'd never escape that prison!"

"But it sure was a good place to hide when our van wrecked," the glider pilot said and laughed. Then he looked at Kurt with a strange expression on his face. "Think our pals who got away in the truck that night will know where we are?"

Kurt knew exactly what he was thinking. "Not a chance! They just know we're all scattered, that's all. What do you have in mind?" he asked with a straight face.

"Well, it just occurred to me that what they don't know won't hurt them. They're probably a long way away. When we didn't join them the next day, they must have thought we'd been captured, especially when the news media told of the robbery and the wreck of the van. They sure don't know how to find us now!"

"So?" Kurt asked. He wanted the man to mention this betrayal of their comrades before he did.

"So, these jewels will make a sizable fortune for all of us, including those at the villa who are in on it. Why should we have to share it with more people?"

Kurt looked at the other men in the helicopter one by one, then said with a straight face, "I'll have to ask them about this."

"You don't have to ask *me*!" the man behind him said with a laugh. "I say we split it with all of us who worked this escape today! Forget those two!"

The other men laughed raucously at this and agreed wholeheartedly.

Kurt grinned and sat back in his seat. "You guys give me no choice," he pretended. "We'll all be richer for this."

Suddenly, the hilarious mood in the helicopter was shattered as the pilot shouted, "We've been sabotaged! Our external tanks are almost empty!"

"What do you mean?" Kurt yelled in reply. "You were supposed to have two full tanks for this flight!"

"We did!" the pilot yelled back. "But they're empty. They were full when we landed. Something's happened! We can't make that rendezvous! We've got to land somewhere else!"

Panicked arguments filled the helicopter as the men reacted to this disastrous news.

CHAPTER 19

HELICOPTERS

Mark and David listened to the now silent woods. After a few minutes, David asked, "Shouldn't we go to the villa and look for Penny?"

"I guess so," Mark said, a worried frown on his face. "But I'd sure hate for those guards to get us from behind as we climb that hill to the house."

"So would I," David agreed. He thought for a minute. "Maybe we could move along the edge of the forest to the left and get away from this spot. We'd be closer to the back of the villa then. Maybe we wouldn't be so visible."

They agreed to do this and began to move silently and carefully through the woods, looking around constantly for the security guards. For 10 minutes, they continued their progress along the edge of the forest. Finally, David stopped and looked at his friend.

"What about heading for the house now?"

"Might as well," Mark agreed. "We can't leave Penny by herself forever. But I've been thinking. Let me go first. You stay behind until I get near the house. That way, if anyone stops me, you won't be caught. Maybe you can get the drop on anyone who stops me, then you can rescue me again!" Mark tried to grin but was too nervous.

David didn't like to let Mark go first, but he knew the plan was a good one. Otherwise they both might be caught at once, and there would be no one to help them or Penny.

"Okay, Let's pray." David said. Both boys prayed silently.

Mark took a deep breath and looked solemn. "Well, here goes," he said.

David stuck out his hand and Mark gripped it. "When you get to the house, make sure it's safe on that end. Then give me a wave, I'll start out."

"Right!" Mark agreed. He turned and began to walk rapidly out of the woods.

David stood, holding his breath as his friend walked into the open. *Did the guards hear us as we moved through the woods? Did they follow us? Would they shout for Mark to stop? And shoot if he didn't?* David's throat was dry as he prayed that the Lord would let Mark reach the house. And that they'd find Penny safe.

Mark moved across the open field feeling terribly visible and vulnerable. Ten yards . . . fifteen . . . twenty. No one shouted for him to stop. No one fired.

Back at the edge of the woods, David released his breath, gulped some air, and tried to relax. Mark was absolutely unprotected, 40 yards away, walking in an apparently relaxed manner, looking to the left and right as if he hadn't a care in the world. But he was moving quickly.

Mark studied the windows and doors of the house as he approached. What would he do if guards came out to stop him? Draw his gun? *That would be suicide!* he thought. If the guards captured him, he'd just have to trust that David would see what happened and find a way to come get him.

Mark was close to the side of the house now. But no one was moving about. Puzzled, he stepped to the back and peered in the kitchen window. No one was in sight. He moved quickly around the wall and waved for David. Then he watched as his friend began his walk from the woods.

Mark's mouth was dry as David left the cover of the woods and moved into the open. He searched the trees behind his friend, praying that none of those guards would emerge and challenge David. It seemed that David was moving in slow motion, but Mark knew he was actually walking as fast as possible.

Farther and farther from the forest David walked, closer and closer to the villa. He walked with his hands in his pockets, seemingly relaxed, but Mark knew David had to be as nervous as he had been! Still, it was a good act. No one watching him would have thought David felt any sense of danger.

Finally, David reached the yard. Then he stepped to the back wall where Mark waited. Mark stuck out his hand with a big grin and David gripped it.

"Thank God!" Mark said.

"I have!" David agreed. "Now let's find Penny!"

Mark stepped to the kitchen door. David followed. They moved through the giant, strangely silent kitchen and entered the wide hall. Side by side now, the friends continued through the back part of the house until they came to the wide cross-way with halls leading to the left into the Brauns' wing and to the right into the guest wing.

Turning toward the guest wing, the young men crept silently along the thickly carpeted floor until they came to Mr. Daring's room.

Mark stopped and whispered to David: "If she's here, she's probably hiding until help comes. I'll go in first. You wait, just in case!"

David nodded.

Mark gripped the door handle, turned it slowly and silently, then, moved like lightning into the room.

"Mark!" Penny cried, as her brother turned to face the strange man who leaped from a chair. "He's a friend! Oh, Mark!" She ran across the room and threw herself into her brother's arms. "Oh, I was so worried about you!" she said through her tears. "Thank God, you're safe!"

She hugged him with all her strength and he hugged her back, thanking the Lord that she'd made it safely to the room.

David heard her cry and stepped into the room, closing the door behind him.

"This is Herr Horning!" Penny told Mark, trying now to be quiet. "He's a friend!" Then she saw David. "Oh, David!" she cried. She rushed to him and threw her arms around his neck. He hugged her back.

Mark greeted Herr Horning. "Did she call the police?" he asked quietly.

"Yes, Mark, she did," the tall gentleman replied. "She thinks they'll be here soon."

"It won't be too soon for me!" Mark said. "This has been quite a day!"

Suddenly, a tremendous noise beat at the windows.

"What's that?" Mark asked, rushing to look out. "Helicopters!" He answered his own question. "But whose?"

David let Penny go, turned and locked the door, then started to join Mark at the window when he realized they didn't really know this man who said his name was Horning. So he remained by the door, keeping his eye on the stranger.

They all listened intently to the increasing noise coming from the sky. Two police helicopters swept over the intervening fields, parted, and landed on opposite sides of the house.

"We'd better wait here in the room until they come searching," Mark suggested.

A minute later, the three teenagers and Herr Horning could hear men rushing through the house.

"I'll unlock and open the door," Mark suggested. He crossed the room and did just that.

"But we don't want to scare those armed men by suddenly appearing in the hall," David warned. "Let's just let them find us."

They all agreed to that. Mark and David had put their guns on the floor behind the bed to be handed to the police. Suddenly, they heard a babble of voices down the hall.

"The police must have released the servants," Herr Horning explained.

Anxiously, they waited for the police to find them. It - didn't take long.

CHAPTER 20

"WE GOT THEM ALL!"

That evening, the dinner in Joseph Braun's villa was a victory celebration. Jim Daring and the three teenagers had been invited to stay with the Schultzes and celebrate with the Brauns the capture of the thieves and the recovery of the stolen jewels. The Brauns and their guests were dressed for the occasion—the men in coats and ties, the ladies in dresses. Penny wore one of her blue dresses that David liked so much.

"We got them!" Joseph Braun exclaimed, his face beaming. "The thieves had been hiding on my property all this time!" He shook his head in disbelief. "And I had such complete faith in my security men! They're the ones who worked out this robbery with the thieves. They released the gas that put us all to sleep so we could be robbed! They sabotaged the security system so that the hang gliders could come over the walls and land in the yard. They let the thieves go through the gate in the van with the jewels, and they hid those glider pilots in the tunnel when their van was wrecked. How could I have been fooled so completely?"

"You did all you could, Joseph," his wife reminded him with a smile. "You can't prevent human nature from giving in to greed and working to betray your trust." She reached over and patted his hand.

"She's right, Joseph," Herr Schultz insisted. "Some men are loyal until they're tempted. Your men had been loyal for years. This temptation was more than they wanted to resist, so they betrayed you."

"But how did the thieves get caught, Herr Braun?" Penny asked, perplexed. "We haven't heard about that."

"I'm not really sure, Penny," their host replied. "That is, I don't know *why* they were caught. I do know how. They'd escaped in a helicopter with hospital markings and were flying low across the countryside, intending to land on a private farm many miles away and transfer to a waiting tour bus. But something happened to their fuel tanks, and they had to land too soon."

"The police said the tanks had been shot to pieces," Herr Schultz added, "but they don't have any idea who did it! They're mystified!"

Penny was surprised to see Mark and David exchange grins. But they didn't say anything, and she wondered what they were thinking. Then she listened as Joseph Braun continued.

"The loss of their fuel forced them to change their plans. They made a hasty decision—a bad decision, as it turned out!—to land at a small airport to the west of us. But Mark and David had already told the police what that helicopter looked like and the direction it took when it left the villa, so the police had put out an alert. As soon as it landed at the airport, the people at the terminal called the police. They were captured a few minutes later with all the jewels in their possession!"

"And they talked!" Herr Schultz said, grinning. "They hoped to get a better deal for themselves, so they told the police how the robbery occurred, how the security guards made it possible, and which of the guards were in on the plan."

"They certainly did talk!" Herr Braun beamed. "They told the police all they needed to know to unravel this whole devilish plot!" He turned to the three teenagers. "But what I want to know is this: How did you three figure it out? Your father told me you'd explained the whole thing to him when the guards lured us out of the villa with false messages. How did you know what had happened?"

"David figured it out, Herr Braun," Penny said. "We were exploring the castle in Königstein, and we found the damaged hang glider hidden in one of the tunnels. Then, when we got to the top of the tower, David found your villa in his binoculars. He realized that it would be an easy flight for gliders from such a height as the castle walls." She beamed proudly at David until his face got red.

"Then we saw the man in the garden signaling someone in the woods," David added. "We knew something was up."

"That's what we wanted to investigate," Mark said. "We told Dad what we suspected, but we wanted to be sure. So we went and looked in the woods."

"And that's where you got in a lot of danger!" Mr. Daring

said to his son. "You boys—and Penny!" he said pointedly.

"Yes, sir," Mark replied. He and David were not proud that they had endangered her.

"But you covered yourself with glory, Mark, when you fought those men and let Penny escape!" his father added. "And you did the same, David, when you rescued Mark. That was great work, and I'm proud of you!"

Mr. Daring turned to his daughter. "And I'm mighty proud of you, young lady, for the way you got to the back of the house, then to my room, so you could signal the police. If you hadn't crawled around that hill, the police wouldn't have been notified in time to catch those thieves! That's why they got here so quickly!"

"And that's how they were able to put out the alert for the escaping helicopter," Herr Braun added. "The police said that in just 10 more minutes those thieves might have escaped!" He smiled gratefully at the three teenagers.

"Well, Jim," Joseph Braun declared, "your young people did a wonderful thing for me and for my friends. And for Anatole Navarre, who's happy to have his jewels back!"

"Actually, Joseph, they've been helping me out all summer," Mr. Daring replied proudly.

Frau Braun rose. "Let's go to the living room for our coffee."

"Would you excuse us, please?" Mark asked his hostess.

"Certainly, Mark," she said and smiled.

Mark, Penny, and David walked out of the room, through the hall, and onto the patio. There was no moon, but hundreds of stars shone in the dark sky.

Penny reached for Mark's strong arm and gave him a hug. He hugged her back and took her hand. She turned and smiled up at David as the three walked into the garden.

"What a summer!" David exclaimed. "My folks thought I'd get to relax with you and your family in East Africa. Instead, I've been running for my life ever since I got off the plane! Don't you people ever *rest*?"

"David, that's not fair, and you know it!" Penny replied, pretending to be indignant. "We lead very quiet lives. We've never—never!—seen so much action! It's all your fault and you know it! Isn't that right, Mark?"

"It sure is, Penny. It sure is. This guy is going to bring us to an early grave. If we live out this summer, that is. No wonder his parents sent him away!"

"Wait a minute!" David protested, taking Penny's other hand in his.

Inside the house, in the living room, the adults were enjoying their coffee.

"Those young people have had quite a time these past two days!" Herr Braun said. "What will you do with the rest of this week, Jim?"

"They really deserve a break," Mr. Daring replied with a grin. "You wouldn't believe the dangers they've encountered this summer! I'm going to let them accept the Schultzes' invitation to spend a few days in Frankfurt and see the sights. They'll get a real rest there, and they can finish their work for me."

"Jim," Frau Schultz said, "have they visited Freiburg? In the Black Forest?"

"No," Mr. Daring replied, "they haven't."

"Then, let me lend them my car so they can go there for a couple of days. It's beautiful countryside. And Freiburg is a fascinating city."

"Why, that's very generous," Jim Daring replied. "I know they'd love to do that. And they certainly shouldn't encounter danger there!"

Awesome Adventures With the Daring Family

Everywhere Mark and Penny Daring and their friend David go, there's sure to be lots of action, mystery and suspense! They often find themselves in the most unpredictable, hair-raising situations. Join them on each of their faith-building voyages in the "Daring Adventure" series as they learn to rely on each other and—most importantly—God!

Ambushed in Africa

An attempted kidnapping! A daring rescue! A breathtaking chase through crocodile-infested waters! Can the trio outwit the criminals before the top secret African diamond mine surveys are stolen?

Trapped in Pharaoh's Tomb

The kids are trapped in an ancient Egyptian tomb. How will they escape before the air runs out? Will they be able to outsmart their rival?

Stalked in the Catacombs

Penny, Mark and David explore Paris . . . but their adversary is lurking in the shadows. Will they be able to outrun him through the dark catacombs beneath the city streets?

Surrounded by the Crossfire

Rival drug smugglers will stop at nothing to get what they want. Why are KGB agents following Penny? Will the kids get caught in the middle of the danger?

Hot Pursuit on the High Seas

The trio is involved in an incredible hunt involving a catamaran, a Russian sub, helicopters and more! Will they find the courage and creativity needed to escape from their predicament?

Hunted Along the Rhine

Tapped phone lines, hidden TV cameras, neo-Nazis and a crossbowman make the kids' assignment for Mr. Daring's company not only difficult, but dangerous! Will they survive a bullet-flying speedboat chase?

Available at your favorite local Christian bookstore.

Breakaway
With colorful graphics, hot topics and humor, this magazine for teen guys helps them keep their faith on course and gives the latest info on sports, music, celebrities ... even girls. Best of all, this publication shows teens how they can put their Christian faith into practice and resist peer pressure.